Playing With Dynamite

The explosion's force hit everyone watching directly in the face. A prehistoric rumble welled up out of the earth's scarred and tortured hide. The clap of doom grew, swelled, and turned into thunder.

The boulder slipped free of its earthly bonds and fell through the air like a gigantic rust-colored cannonball. It rocketed through Calico Jack's roof like a Comanche war spear. The cabin exploded in a cyclone of flying wreckage.

Longarm heeled it around the protective boulders for a closer look. The others assembled in an amazed knot of pointing, chin scratching, head shaking, and mumbled commentary.

Mike Rader gazed up at the mushroom-shaped cloud of thick, red dust. "That's got to be the damnedest thing I've ever seen in my entire life."

Stewart Potts yelled, "Got any more of that dynamite, Marshal Long? Maybe we could set off another stick or three just for the fun of it."

"Helluva performance you done put on for us today, Marshal," said Skunk Hornbuckle. "Bet folks'll be tellin' this tale for years to come. I ain't never even heard of nuthin' to match 'er."

Then, to everyone's slack-jawed bewilderment and total surprise, a singular and stunning miracle occurred. Calico Jack Blackman stumbled out of the billowing waves of dust . . . like a ghostly performer in a traveling magician's show . . .

TABOR EVANS

LONGARM

IN HELL'S HALF ACRE

JOVE BOOKS, NEW YORK

THE BERKLEY PUBLISHING GROUP
Published by the Penguin Group
Penguin Group (USA) Inc.
375 Hudson Street, New York, New York 10014, USA
Penguin Group (Canada), 90 Eglinton Avenue East, Suite 700, Toronto, Ontario M4P 2Y3, Canada
(a division of Pearson Penguin Canada Inc.)
Penguin Books Ltd., 80 Strand, London WC2R 0RL, England
Penguin Group Ireland, 25 St. Stephen's Green, Dublin 2, Ireland (a division of Penguin Books Ltd.)
Penguin Group (Australia), 250 Camberwell Road, Camberwell, Victoria 3124, Australia
(a division of Pearson Australia Group Pty. Ltd.)
Penguin Books India Pvt. Ltd., 11 Community Centre, Panchsheel Park, New Delhi—110 017, India
Penguin Group (NZ), 67 Apollo Drive, Rosedale, North Shore 0632, New Zealand
(a division of Pearson New Zealand Ltd.)
Penguin Books (South Africa) (Pty.) Ltd., 24 Sturdee Avenue, Rosebank, Johannesburg 2196,
South Africa

Penguin Books Ltd., Registered Offices: 80 Strand, London WC2R 0RL, England

This is a work of fiction. Names, characters, places, and incidents either are the product of the author's imagination or are used fictitiously, and any resemblance to actual persons, living or dead, business establishments, events, or locales is entirely coincidental.

LONGARM IN HELL'S HALF ACRE

A Jove Book / published by arrangement with the author

PRINTING HISTORY
Jove edition / November 2007

Copyright © 2007 by The Berkley Publishing Group.
Cover illustration by Miro Sinovcic.

ISBN: 978-0-515-14371-3

JOVE®
Jove Books are published by The Berkley Publishing Group,
a division of Penguin Group (USA) Inc.,
375 Hudson Street, New York, New York 10014.
JOVE is a registered trademark of Penguin Group (USA) Inc.
The "J" design is a trademark belonging to Penguin Group (USA) Inc.

PRINTED IN THE UNITED STATES OF AMERICA

10 9 8 7 6 5 4 3 2 1

Chapter 1

Along the rugged west bank of the Purgatoire River, nigh twenty miles south of Bent's Old Fort, Longarm flipped the top-most layer of his bedroll aside. He rubbed sleep from his eyes with the back of one hand, pushed his snuff-colored Stetson down tight on his head, then plucked a foot-long stick from the dirt.

The droopy-eyed deputy U.S. marshal swayed to unsteady feet from the grasping comfort afforded by his still comfortably warm ground pallet, stretched a kinked spine like a recently awakened bear, then bent over and poked at the embers of a rekindled campfire. A sparkling stream of cold, clear water rushed headlong toward the south a mere thirty yards from the campsite.

Longarm grimaced, while coming fully erect again, then cast a quick, unconcerned glance toward the dark, hairy-faced man in leg irons who hobbled up a section of the river's rocky embankment. A soot-covered, sloshing coffeepot was precariously balanced between the man's grimy, grit-encrusted hands.

"Hurry the hell up with the water, Skunk," Longarm

yelled. "I'm in serious need of a good shot a up-and-at-'em juice. Swear to Jesus, you musta been born tired and raised lazy. Your drag-assed ways are throwin' an inconvenient hitch in my mornin' devotions, you bank-robbin' son of a bitch."

Elroy "Skunk" Hornbuckle's musical leg shackles clinked and jingled as he half-stepped to Longarm's side. The red-eyed prisoner stumbled to a stop like an unwashed pile of varmint-infested rags atop a pair of drunken legs. He grunted, then spat, "If'n I'd a knowed I's gonna end up bein' the sorely abused manservant to a badge-totin' hard-ass like you, Marshal Custis Fuckin' Long, might not a done 'er. Yessir, I'd a given serious thought to passin' on that unfortunate piece a bullet-riddled business I done got led into, like a innocent child, up in Glenwood Springs. Yes, by God, I surely would've."

Hornbuckle slapped the charred tin pot onto the blue-tinted flames. Some of the liquid sloshed from beneath the dented vessel's lid and onto the superheated cinders. The coals hissed, popped, and sent a cloud of steam billowing into Longarm's face. Hornbuckle snorted with delight at his captor's discomfort. He stifled a sniggering laugh behind the back of a grubby paw.

Longarm gritted his teeth, wiped at one eye for a second, then squatted. He pulled fresh coffee from his possibles bag and dumped the required amount of dark, aromatic grounds into the pot and flipped the lid closed. As he rocked back on his heels, he fished around till several stringy sticks of rock-hard beef jerky presented themselves from the canvas sack's murky depths. Much like feeding a stray dog, he pitched a piece of the leathery stuff to his smelly captive.

2

"Gonna take a few minutes for them grounds to boil up, so I'd appreciate it if you'd stand somewhere over on the other side of the fire, Skunk. Odiferous bouquet of stinkweed and polecat you're so freely puttin' off ain't doin' a thing toward makin' this whole dance any more palatable. You're a-layin' a serious reekin' on a damned fine mornin'. Take all these flies with you."

Hornbuckle gnawed off a chunk of the petrified meat. "Right tasty," he mumbled between slobbery efforts to chew. He shook his head like an old wolf with a flea in its ear, then said, "What the fuck do pa-lat-able mean. Pa-lat-able. That some kinda insult? Sounds like a insult to me, by God. Hell's eternal fires, Long, you done went and whacked me on the noggin with yer pistol barrel. Gonna offend me now as well?"

For the first time that morning, Longarm cracked a toothy smile. "Still astonishes me, no end, what some people find to worry over. You could give a rat's ass about me sayin' in no uncertain terms, you stink, but you don't want me usin' words you don't understand—that it, Skunk? Now get the hell over on the other side of the fire. Jesus, my nose hairs are turnin' into corkscrews."

Hornbuckle puffed up like an insulted south Louisiana bullfrog, then shuffled his way to the newly assigned spot. He flopped down atop a convenient rock on the side of the fire nearest the tree line. As if lost in concentration, he stared at passing clouds, then nodded to himself and said, "Damned right, Long. They's folks as claim I been puttin' off a smell 'bout like a wet dog what's been set afire fer as far back as I can 'member.

"Don't surprise me one bit."

"Well, by God, I could care less what any a you perfumed and pomaded bastards think 'bout how I smells.

3

But it do make me some hot when them as think they's so high and mighty wanna talk words where I cain't figure out what they's a sayin'. Pa-lat-able. Ain't never heerd a pa-lat-able afore. If'n I wasn't hobbled up like some kinda field-workin' farm animal, I'd sure 'nuff try and kick yer ass, Mr. Deputy U.S. Marshal Custis Fuckin' Long."

Longarm poked around in the fire with his stick. "Well, other than smellin' like the backside of an outhouse door, you got no reason to be offended, Skunk. Palatable just means I can't take the aroma waftin' off your scruffy ass—leastways not this early in the mornin'."

Hornbuckle threw his head back and laughed. "All a you lawdogs is just a bunch of candy asses, fer as I ever been able to tell." As though to himself, he aimed a twitching nose at the air that hovered around him, lifted an arm, sniffed, then mumbled, "Hell, I don't smell so bad—today. Sure I've smelt worse afore."

When the coffee took on the thick appearance of something akin to axle grease, Longarm poured two cups and gingerly passed one to his captive. Then he settled back into his bedroll and tried to enjoy the sights, the smells other than Skunk Hornbuckle, and the tastes of a glorious spring morning.

A bit of snow still decorated the ground in shaded spots here and there, but some of the trees had begun to bud out and a few multicolored wildflowers bloomed in seemingly random spots near the water. The welcome aroma of coming spring hovered in the air and almost drowned out the stench oozing off Skunk Hornbuckle's malodorous hide.

A few minutes of pleasant, peaceful silence passed, but all of a sudden, Hornbuckle hopped to his feet, tilted his bearlike head to one side, and cupped a hand over an ear that looked like someone had once tried to remove it with a ball-peen hammer.

"You hear that, Marshal?" he hissed. "They's somebody a-comin' through them trees over yonder ways. Couple of 'em—sounds like. Maybe more."

"Been hearin' 'em for about ten minutes, Skunk. Figure they're just about ready to show."

Longarm sat his cup on the log he'd put to his back the night before, then grabbed the Winchester propped against the saddle he'd used as a pillow to rest his weary head. He thumbed the hammer back on the rifle, laid it in his bedding, then flipped the blanket over the weapon in an effort to hide the big repeater.

He slipped the double-action, Frontier model Colt from its cross-draw holster, cocked the weapon, then crossed his arms and slid the pistol-filled hand inside his jacket as though warming the hidden hand. He'd barely gotten comfortable again when a pair of riders urged their animals out of the dense timber, less than a hundred feet down the brush-choked tree line.

One of the riders rose in his stirrups, waved his hat, and called out, "Hello, the camp. Hello the camp. Coffee smells mighty good, gents. Can we approach?"

The sudden realization that he stood between Longarm's weapons and the strangers appeared to hit Skunk Hornbuckle like a fist. The stinky, filth-encrusted thief grunted like a scared porker, ducked his head, and jingled to a spot behind his captor's log.

With his free hand, Longarm waved the riders forward,

then retrieved his cup and assumed the look of a man not the least concerned by the unexpected turn of events.

The tallest of the two strangers, broad in the shoulder and narrow of hip, stepped down first. He pushed back his gray felt hat and exposed an open, friendly face framed by gold-colored hair and decorated with a massive handlebar chin tickler. In what Longarm took as an effort to put the campers at their ease, the man led his long-legged blood bay up to the site rather than ride in.

Longarm's studied gaze flicked from one rider to the other as the tall man's younger companion climbed off his animal and followed suit. Soon enough, both men hunkered near the fire, produced their own cups, and sipped at the freshly brewed, steaming hot belly wash.

"Mighty fine stuff," the moustache said, then sucked at his fluffy whiskers and saluted Longarm with his battered cup. "Right neighborly of you to invite us in. Needed somethin' to warm us up, sir. Been in the saddle since before the crack of dawn."

Longarm's concentrated gaze flitted back and forth from one man to the other. Both strangers carried sidearms strapped high on their waists, but neither made any move to pull his coat away from his weapon. After a minute or so of silence, he said, "What're you boys doin' way out here in the big cold and lonely? Me'n ole Skunk thought we had the whole world to ourselves this mornin'."

The tall man pulled his coat lapel aside long enough to reveal a five-pointed star, then said, "Well, it's like this: My name's Harley Court, mister. I'm the city marshal up in Hadleyville." He hooked a thumb in the direction of his younger companion. "This here's my deputy, Rudy Crabtree. We done chased a soulless, murderin' back shooter by the name of Calico Jack Blackman up into Wild Horse Canyon, few miles down river from here. He went an' burrowed up like a Rocky Mountain tick in a log cabin way in the back of that rugged slash in the earth's tortured hide. Damned place is like a log fort, settin' flush up agin' the canyon's back wall."

Longarm took a sip from his still-steaming cup. "Calico Jack Blackman, huh? Well, you boys done picked a bad'un to be a chasin', Marshal Court. Calico Jack's 'bout as evil of a son of a bitch as they get. Couldn't tempt him to come on out and throw up his hands, I don't expect."

Deputy Rudy Crabtree cast a bemused, gap-toothed smile at the back of Marshal Court's head. One of his thumb-sized front teeth wiggled like it might fall out. "Hell, we couldn't even get close to the place. That there cabin's on a mound of dirt. Kinda raises it up above everthang. He wuz a shootin' down on us from gun slits 'tween the logs." The deputy touched his flapping tooth, then continued, "Laughin' like a thing insane the whole time, he wuz. Couldn't even get a shot at his horse. Had the animal in a sheltered corral 'round behind the cabin. Tough nut to crack, mister. Real tough."

Court appeared to relax. He shifted out of the squat, sat flat on the ground, then leaned over on one elbow like a man tired to the bone. "Left three of my other posse members back yonder, to keep ole Jack occupied. Me'n Rudy 'uz on our way back to town. Thought to raise some more fellers. Come on back quick as we could. But, the more I think on the deal, it might be a total waste of time and effort."

"How so?" Longarm asked.

"Well, ole Jack'll probably figure out he's dealing with clerks, bartenders, and stable hands sooner or later.

Shoot his way past my boys. Be gone by the time we can make it all the way back out here again." He waved absently at the whole countryside in general, then let the arm flop down against his side.

Longarm tapped the side of his cup with one finger. "Now be at ease, gents. Just want to show you somethin'." He pushed his coat open with his free hand and pulled out the wallet containing all his official credentials. When he flipped the leather cover aside, the polished, silver deputy U.S. marshal's badge glittered in the morning sunlight. "My name's Custis Long, Marshal Court. I work out of Denver. And I must admit that I've had occasion to chase Calico Jack around the countryside a time or two myself."

Court's lopsided grin widened into a broad smile. He shook his head. "Just be damned. Now ain't this somethin' of a wonderment, Rudy? What're the chances we'd fall in with other lawmen, way the hell out here in the middle of nowheres, Colorado? Good Lord musta took a likin' to us today."

Skunk Hornbuckle took offense. The fettered thief leapt to his feet and snapped, "Lawmen? Did you say lawmen? Hell's fuckin' bells, I ain't no lawman." He snatched the chain to his leg irons up and shook it at Hadleyville's smiling marshal. "And I want you bastards to know that Calico Jack be a dear friend of mine. Man's the salt of the earth, fer as I'm concerned. Finer feller cain't be found in these parts."

Rudy Crabtree's face went scarlet. "Well, your dear friend rode into our peaceful little town few days back, mister." His voice sounded like a dull saw going through hard wood. "Went and robbed the only hardware and im-

8

plement dealership as we've got. Shot the owner deader'n Abe Lincoln, right in front of his poor shocked wife."

"Musta had a reason fer such a killin'," Skunk grumped.

"That ain't the half of what he done," Crabtree snapped back. "Just for what appeared the sheer hell of it, he trampled a child to death with that fire-breathin', star-faced, black-as-the-depths-of-hell horse of his'n on the way outta town. Don't know 'bout anyone else as might have an opinion on the subject, but I'd say you need to be a-pickin' your friends with a bit more care."

Hornbuckle looked sheepish. His chin dropped to his chest. For a second, he swayed like an aspen struck by lightning. His lips moved several times, but no words came out. Finally, he flopped back down behind the sheltering log, silently stared at the ground, and went to picking at the grass like a chastised child.

Longarm locked Marshal Court in a steely-eyed gaze and said, "You think a stick, or two, of dynamite could shake Calico Jack loose? Maybe persuade him to give himself up? You know, it'd be quite a catch if we could drop a loop over a murderous desperado like him."

Another big smile cut across Court's face from ear to ear. "That's one of the reasons I 'uz on my way to town. Hoped to bring enough explosives back to blast ole Jack outta his hidey-hole. By God, if you've got some already, Marshal Long, and we can get close enough to do any damage at all, I'd give your plan a fifty-fifty chance of workin'."

With the hand still hidden inside his coat, Longarm slipped the pistol back into its holster, then stood and brushed off his pants. "Well, Harley, I've got the dynamite. Let's slip on down the river, see if we can't blast ole Calico Jack out of Wild Horse Canyon. 'Bout time a party of irate citizens put a noose around his sorry neck. Be my distinct pleasure any day of the week to take part in that happy effort."

Skunk Hornbuckle jumped to his feet. "This mean you gonna let me go, Long?"

Longarm glared at the thief as though he'd just seen a freak in a traveling carnival sporting two heads. "Have you lost what little mind you had a few minutes ago, Skunk? Put this fire out, then pack up our stuff and get your stinkin' ass on a horse. We're going to Wild Horse Canyon, you stupid son of a bitch."

Rudy Crabtree burst into cackling laughter and couldn't stop smiling while Hornbuckle took ten minutes to get everything gathered up. In pretty short order, the party of lawmen, with one varmint in tow, were headed south for an appointment with bloody fate.

Chapter 2

Five miles south, on a tortured path along the crystalline river, Longarm followed as Marshal Harley Court turned the posse west into the V-shaped opening of a tight gash in the earth. The ground beneath their animals' feet gently sloped for about a hundred yards, then leveled out inside a narrow gorge flanked by steep walls of bloodred earth and sun-bleached boulders the size of a Concord coach. The floor of the craggy, rock-strewn gulch was center split by a sparkling, shallow creek that shimmered in the sparse sunlight filtering in from above.

"If a man didn't know the exact location of Wild Horse Canyon, he might never know it existed," Longarm muttered to himself as he gazed up and down the chasm's rugged sixty-foot walls.

Stunted, leaf-heavy trees grew in dense profusion on either side of the close-feeling trail. Thick undergrowth added to Longarm's growing sense of restricted movement. With a shrug, he tried to throw off the creeping, urgent desire for open space.

The party punched into the overgrowth for nigh half

11

a mile, as nearly as Longarm could figure it. Then, all of a sudden, the chasm opened up to an unhampered breadth of almost 150 yards across. A mere sixty or so yards out of the tress and scrub, he could see a string of boulders resting at the base of a small hill, or mound, so perfectly formed it appeared man-made.

Atop the abbreviated rise, another hundred yards past the row of sheltering rocks, Longarm spotted the barely visible pole roof of a cabin. From his less-than-helpful vantage point, the rough, crudely erected abode appeared to stand flush against the back wall of the ravine.

A bit over halfway between the cabin and the posse's naturally occurring shelter, a single monolithic spire of granite jutted from the earth like a giant's extended finger. At the base of the hill, safely behind the column of boulders, men and horses had gathered around a smoky fire near the largest of the massive stones.

The logistical problems caused by the terrain, along with the log shack's virtually unassailable location, were glaringly obvious to even the most inexperienced man chaser, Longarm thought. He did a quick, reasoned assessment of the situation. He knew exactly what had to be done and, more importantly, how to go about doing it.

Marshal Court reined in his blood bay and stepped down as two men left their smoky fire and rushed up to him. A fat-gutted citizen wearing a derby hat, ratty fur coat, and run-down shoes yelped, "Jesus, Harley, this is the best you could do? Two men was all what could come out and help? Ain't no improvement a'tall, far as I can see. Hell, we're confronted with a man killer up yonder. Gonna need least more'n five men to pry him loose."

Court slapped leather reins against his gloved palm, shifted from foot to foot, then motioned toward Longarm as the Denver lawman dismounted. "Yeah, well Mike, only one of 'em is here to actually help. But we got a good'un. And he brung some dynamite. Soon's we blast Calico Jack outta his nest, we can all go home, and you can get back to slinging drinks and a-tryin' to look down Sissy Lovelace's dress all day at them big ole tits of hers."

The second of Court's posse men was a rail-thin, yellow-skinned, skull-faced creature that jerked and shook like he had a colony of scorpions in his pants. The man had the haggard appearance of someone who suffered from a debilitating bout of something a bit more than unpleasant. Longarm assessed it as a combination of several types of venereal disease, and the lingering effects of a bout with malaria.

Court waved Longarm to his side and said, "Marshal Long, this here is Mike Rader. Runs the Queen of Hearts Saloon in Hadleyville. Squirmy feller's Stewart Potts. Stew's a horse wrangler for our local blacksmith."

Longarm tipped his hat. "Gents."

Both men nodded back, but neither seemed inclined toward anything like an overtly friendly display. Rader had the look of a man on the verge of passing out, while Potts appeared ready for the next world. *They're scared,* Longarm thought, *so panic-struck they can barely function.*

Rader grumped, "What about t' other'un? The ugly son of a bitch." He strolled a bit too close to Hornbuckle, shook his head, held his nose, and yelped, "Shit almighty, feller. Don't you ever bathe? Stink like somethin' dead. Smell like you just crawled outta a wolf's den. Met up with a feller one time who had a wet goat under each arm what didn't give off the stench you're puttin' out."

"He's my prisoner," Longarm offered. "We were on our way back to the federal lockup in Denver when we met up with Marshal Court."

Rader moved as far from Hornbuckle as he could get and still be part of the conversational circle. "Well, Jesus, even that don't give him the right to stink like he's been sleepin' in a stock pen."

Harley Court's head swiveled around on his thin neck. He gazed into every shaded spot and sheltered corner of the canyon. "Where's Gabe, boys?" he asked.

Potts scratched his scraggly, stubble-covered chin with a trembling hand, then glanced at the back of Rader's head as though looking for guidance he didn't get. "Well, see, Harley, it's like this. Gabe done went and skipped out on us. Said he'd had enough of such nonsense. Ask me, he ain't been the same since he almost got nailed the day we arrived. Headed back for town's what he done. Didn't you see him on your way back out here?"

"No." Court shook his head. "Most likely he didn't want me to see him, Stew. But you know, to tell the God's truth, I can understand his feelings. Man just got married a few weeks ago. Guess he figured he might go and get himself kilt out here, if'n this dance went the wrong way. Don't really matter, I suppose. This party's gonna end pretty quick when we blast ole Jack outta his hidey-hole."

Longarm strode back to his mount, flipped up the flap on his saddle bag, and dragged out three thick sticks of scarlet-colored dynamite and a small metal box. The other men gathered around to watch. He squatted, laid the explosives on the ground in a neat row, then removed an equal number of detonators and a length of fuse from the tin container. Once he had everything properly prepared for deadly use, he stood and examined his work one last time.

"Looks good, Marshal Long," Court offered. "But how're we gonna get even one of 'em up there close enough to do any real damage? Cain't throw 'em that far. Ain't a blade of grass 'tween safety behind these rocks and the cabin's front door, 'cept that one piece of granite yonder. A man could seek shelter there, I suppose. Get him a bit closer to the cabin 'thout getting killed graveyard dead. But he'd still be fifty yards away from our target."

Longarm pointed toward the rim of the canyon wall. "Someone's gonna have to make his way up above and drop 'em right down on ole Jack's head, while those who remain down here set up a commotion to distract him." He turned to Rudy Crabtree. "Think you can do that, Deputy? Think you could claw your way up to the top yonder and drop these blasters on the cabin's roof?"

For a moment, Harley Court's second in command looked somewhat flustered and confused, but he gathered himself up, shrugged, and said, "Suppose so, Marshal Long. Yeah, I think I could do 'er. Just one problem though."

Longarm grinned. "And what might that be, Rudy?"

"Ain't never handled no dynamite afore. Ain't never even been close enough to touch a stick of the stuff, till this very minute."

"Nothin' to it," Longarm said, in as gentle and reassuring a manner as he could muster. Then, he held one of the flame-colored sticks up in the boy's face. "All you gotta do, Rudy, is put fire to the fuse, and then get it onto the roof of the cabin. Stuff ain't nothin' more'n a big firecracker. I've cut the fuses long enough to give you at least ten seconds to get rid of the charge once it's lit. Only real problem you should have is finding your way up there to a likely spot on the canyon rim. Near as I can figure, you'll probably have to go back out the entrance, then pick your way to the top afoot. Might well take most of the day."

Crabtree's gaze shifted from the dynamite in Longarm's hand and slid along the canyon wall and up to the spot above Calico Jack's bulletproof fortress. He nodded as though to himself, then scratched the back of his head. "Guess I'd best get started then, hadn't I?"

Longarm laid the charged explosives on a rough-cut square of burlap from his saddlebag. He wrapped the cloth into a neat package, tied it with a piece of twine, then handed it to the deputy. "Just don't drop 'em, Rudy," he said. "Try not to accidentally bash 'em up against anything. Them detonators are sensitive and prone to explode if abused in any fashion whatsoever. You understand, son?"

Crabtree nodded, as though in a trance, took the rough parcel, gingerly slipped it into the saddlebag on his own animal, then climbed aboard. He grasped the reins between fingers that trembled and said, "Guess I'd best get goin'. I'll fire a shot from the rim, wave my hat or somethin', soon's I get situated in a place where I think I can do the most damage. So you boys be on the lookout. Don't want to surprise you by settin' this stuff off 'fore you're ready."

Longarm slapped the boy on the leg. "Sounds good.

Just be careful. This ugly hairball's gonna work out just fine once you drop one of those big poppers on Calico Jack's head."

Longarm, Marshal Court, and his remaining posse, along with an increasingly antsy Skunk Hornbuckle, watched until Deputy Rudy Crabtree disappeared into the trees back up the overgrown trail toward the Purgatoire.

Court snatched off his hat and slapped his leg with it. He shrugged, stuffed the hat back on, then said, "Well, whatta we do now, Marshal Long?"

Longarm turned. He gazed around the campsite, along behind the line of sheltering boulders, up to the cabin and the canyon wall, then back to the campsite. "We spread out behind these rocks and, every once in a while, take a potshot at Jack's log-and-mud sanctuary. Just to keep him on his toes. Make him think somethin's about to happen. Want the man nervous and expectant."

"Hell, we already been a-doin' that all along," Rader grumped, then levered a live round into the chamber of his Winchester.

"And he usually answers back with a well-aimed blast of his own," Potts added. "Murderin' son of a bitch ain't took no stuff off'n us, so far, Marshal Long. He's got the high ground and knows it. That's for damned sure. Go and stick your head out from behind any of these rocks, and he'll blow it off. Man's a helluva good shot, if'n you ask me."

"Any place where I can safely get a look?" Longarm asked.

Court pointed to a spot behind a split boulder secluded behind several leaning cottonwoods. "Over there, Marshal. Don't think he can see through the leaves. You get a pretty good view up the slope."

Longarm snatched the army surplus binoculars off his saddle and started for the trees. As he passed Skunk Hornbuckle, he stopped and said, "Took them leg irons off and put you in handcuffs so you could ride a horse, Skunk. Now I'm gonna take these irons off your wrists so you can have coffee and take care of your twa-let, if necessary. But try to run on me and you know what'll happen, don't you?"

Hornbuckle rubbed his wrists, hung his head, then grumbled, "Yeah, yeah, yeah, Long, I know. You'll shoot the hell outta me. Make damned sure I'm pushin' up bluebonnets 'fore the sun goes down. Don't have to go a-worryin' yerself none on my account. I ain't a-goin' nowheres." The outlaw glanced at his confined surroundings, then said, "Country 'round these parts is so cramped and rough, I probably wouldn't get a hundred feet 'fore you kilt me deader'n a drowned cat."

Longarm heeled it for the trees. Over his shoulder he snapped, "Good thinkin', Skunk. Mr. Rader, you and Mr. Potts find a nice spot. Throw a few shots up Jack's way. Blue whizzer or two here and there'll do just fine. No need to waste ammunition. Just want a get him stirred up a bit."

A few minutes later, with Harley Court breathing down his neck, Longarm leaned against the base of a thick-trunked, low-limbed cottonwood and adjusted his view through the field glasses. The image finally came into focus and something odd popped up. "What're those dark mounds scattered around the slope goin' up the hill?"

Court let out an exasperated sigh. "Dead dogs. We counted three, maybe four. Could be more. Figured they either set up a racket when Calico Jack approached, or maybe he got tired of their barkin' once he got inside and decided to put an end to it. No way to tell for certain."

Longarm backed away from the tree and turned to face Court. "Dogs? Damn. Takes one sorry son of a bitch to shoot a defenseless dog, for no good reason. Killin' three or four of 'em like that's just downright, good for nothin', low-life crazy. Damnation, I'd rather tie a double knot in a mountain lion's tail than have to deal with a man who's snapped a link in his trace chain. Calico Jack's never been known as the most dependable boat on the river, but I really didn't know him as crazy."

"My sentiments exactly, Marshal Long. But the situation confronting us, at the moment, is what it is. Just gonna have to deal with it."

For a second, Longarm's brow knotted and a pained look flitted across his weathered face. A spark of realization lit his eyes like a Fourth of July whizbang. "Damn, Harley," he said, "if there's dead dogs up on the hill, near the cabin, that means there's probably people. You think there's any possibility that we might have other folks inside that hovel with Calico Jack?"

Court peered up through the tree limbs, then toed the ground. "Well, we're pretty sure there *mighta been* at least one other man in the cabin when Jack stormed in and took over the place."

"You're pretty sure? Is that anything like *kinda definite*? Do you have anything substantial to base that opinion on?"

Hadleyville's marshal cast an eye-blinking glance at the patch of cloud-filled, crystal blue sky above them, then shook his head. "Not really. Look, Marshal Long, when we first got here, my man Gabe Coldwell, the one who hotfooted it back to Hadleyville, made it most of the way up the hill 'fore any shootin' got cranked up good. He come nigh on gettin' himself kilt, right then and there. Once we got back down here behind cover, he told me as how it appeared to him there mighta been a man's body stretched out on the ground right outside the front door. That'd explain the biscuit eaters."

Longarm kicked at a rock with the heel of his boot. "Well, yeah, maybe that'd explain the dogs," he snapped. He ran a hand to the back of his neck. He twisted his head sideways till he could feel the bones pop. "Jeez, just had a horrible thought."

"What? What'd you think, Marshal?"

"What if there's a woman up there, Harley? Christ, just think of that. Shit, we can't stop Rudy now. It's too late. He's gonna blow that place to powder 'fore the day's out."

Chapter 3

Marshal Harley Court wagged his head back and forth, then toed at some of the rocks on the ground. "Damn. Captives? Maybe a woman? Never even gave that likelihood a moment's thought, Marshal Long."

"Well, you shoulda, Harley. Shoulda told me about your suspicions soon as I pulled all that dynamite outta my saddlebag. Men in our position can't make mistakes like this. We might all end up responsible for the untimely death of a woman, and sweet Jesus, perhaps even children, for all we know. Ain't that a horrific thought?"

Court looked stricken when he said, "Children? Christ Almighty, don't think they's children up there, do you, Long?"

Longarm cast a worried glance back toward Calico Jack's stronghold. "Reckon we can talk to him? Did you, or any of your people, try to feel him out a bit before you started back to Hadleyville for help?"

"Sure. 'Course we tried. He can hear us just fine. Fact is, I've come to think that sound kinda creeps up his way, somehow. Echo in this place can be damned near deafening when we're pourin' lead in on him. Yeah, I figure

21

ole Jack hears damned near everything we do and most of what gets said. Willing to bet you the piddling six dollars in my wallet he already knows someone else has showed up to help us bring him to book."

"Well, that might be stretchin' it a mite."

"No. Don't think so, Marshal Long. We shouted up first chance that presented itself. Tried to get him to come out. Told him he'd be safe if he gave it up. Longer we talked, the louder the son of a bitch laughed. Pitched more and more lead our direction ever' time I opened my mouth."

"He never called out and said anything about a hostage?"

"Nothin' 'bout no hostages. I swear it. Not a single word. 'Course, he swore at us in the ugliest kinda language he could lay his tongue to. Accordin' to ole Jack, every one of us boys from Hadleyville is either a motherfucker or a cocksucker or a puss-covered anal sphincter of some kind or related by birth to some form of stinkin' human waste."

A toothy grin spread across Longarm's face. "Sounds like you boys got an earful."

"Hell, that's not the half of it. On top of the constant stream of scabrous lip, the murderin' wretch musta fired off near a hundred rounds that first day we had him pinned down. Surprised the hell outta me he had that much ammunition available to burn up. We could hear him screechin' and laughin' like a loon, shootin' off his guns and such, but I swear, he never offered to talk and there was no mention a'tall about other folks bein' up there."

The tension appeared to drain from Longarm's face. "Well, maybe we're okay, Harley. But it might still be a good idea to try and feel him out a bit. Think I just might try and get him to come out and palaver for a spell. Can't hurt."

The words had barely tumbled from Longarm's lips when Rader and Potts cut loose and peppered the hilltop hideout with a hailstorm of lead. Longarm glanced up at the cabin's heavy front facade and watched as flying chunks of splintered timber and dusty ricochets worked to obscure the posse's view. Within minutes, the stagnant air at the bottom of the canyon reeked with the acrid smell of spent black powder. Dense gray clouds of drifting gunsmoke hovered overhead.

The unhurried shelling continued as Longarm strolled back to the campfire, poured a cup of coffee from the posse's pot, then sat down on a rock and pulled a cheroot from his vest pocket. He lit the cigar and took his time smoking it, while nursing the tin of overcooked stump juice. Marshal Court poured a cup as well, but spent his time moving back and forth from one of his men to the other. He talked, patted them on their backs, and encouraged their efforts.

With his last drag on the smoldering, mangled cheroot stub, Longarm stood and called out to Rader and Potts, "That's enough, fellers. Wanna let ole Jack chew on his predicament for a spell. If he don't respond, call out or somethin', then maybe we'll start up again when Rudy shows himself on the canyon wall."

For about ten minutes, the inside of Wild Horse Canyon got quieter than a deaf-mute's shadow. Then, all of a sudden, as though from the bottom of an enormous metal barrel, Longarm barely heard someone say, "That you down there, Long? Seen you come in. Watched everthang you boys done through my long glass. If'n I'd a had my Big Fifty in hand, couple of you fellers would already be dancin' with Jesus."

Harley Court whispered, "See what I meant? Damn. Can you believe that? Sounds like he's sittin' right here in camp with us."

Longarm hustled from the fireside, pressed himself against the nearest boulder, then snatched a fleeting peek up the slope. He cupped his hands around his mouth and yelled, "That you, Jack?"

Somewhere up above, Longarm could scarcely make out a man's laughter. Then, louder the second time, he heard, "'Course it's me, you stupid, law-bringin' cocksucker. Who'd you think it was? Jesse Fuckin' James?"

In spite of himself, Longarm smiled. He called out, "Need to get yourself on down here, Jack. Gonna be hell to pay if you don't."

"Well, now, that's a hoot. Hell to pay if'n I don't. Shit. Hell to pay if'n I do, too. Oh, I know you boys is up to somethin'. Just cain't figure exactly what. Seen that feller leave a while back. That don't mean I'm a gonna give it up. Hangman's a-waitin' for me, Long, and you know it. Law cain't wait to stretch my neck. Think I'd rather die here, maybe take some of y'all with me, than shit my britches in front of a buncha drunk gawkers."

"No need to make the situation any worse, Jack. Might go and get yourself, or one of these other men, killed for sure if you keep this up. Just come on down. You know me. I'll treat you right."

Tinny laughter filtered down from the cabin. "Yeah, bet you would. You know, Long, I seen you a year or so back. You was there when they hung Squeaky Evans from the gallows up in Carbondale."

24

"I remember, Jack. Nasty business. Squeaky murdered a parlor house whore up that way. Cut her throat with a straight razor. Damn near took her head off."

"Yeah, well a man shouldn't have to die in such an unsightly manner for murderin' no parlor house whore. Folks talked it around that you was the one what caught ole Squeaky and brought him back to swing. You 'member how that poor man messed hisself right in front of nigh on a thousand people, Long? I do. Ain't lettin' nothin' even approachin' that ever happen to me. You sons of bitches gonna have to kill ole Calico Jack right here in Wild Horse Canyon."

Red-faced and shaking, Marshal Court yelled, "We can damned sure bury you here, or you can come on down and give yourself up. Either way, you ain't leavin' this place a free man. Killed people in my town, you son of a bitch, and I'm takin' you back, one way or the other." Cackling laughter was the answer to Court's tirade.

"Come on up here and get me, you badge-totin' bastards. Ain't none of you yeller bellys got balls big enough to slap chains on Calico Jack Blackman."

The mouthy outlaw followed his challenge with a pair of well-placed rifle shots that splattered shards of broken rock all over Longarm and Hadleyville's angry marshal. Court gritted his teeth, then spat, when broken stone and dust decorated his face. Rader and Potts cut loose with another harmless volley that did little more than make a lot of unneeded, booming racket.

Following a number of similar exchanges, the afternoon settled into relative quiet. As the sun got higher and the day seemed to get longer and sweatier, Longarm made himself a nest, lay down, and drifted off into a much-needed nap. He awoke, pulled out his Ingersoll railroader's watch, and checked the time. As he snapped the case shut and slid the timepiece back into his vest pocket, Stewart Potts hustled over and pulled him to his feet. Everyone in camp appeared mesmerized by something. The agitated deputy pointed to the canyon wall above the cabin.

"Be damned," Longarm whispered. "Rudy actually made it. And he done it damned quick, too."

Beside a massive boulder, perched precariously on the gorge's rim, Rudy Crabtree leapt up and down and waved his hat. "Everyone wave back," Longarm said. "Want the boy to know we've spotted him."

For some seconds, the entire party tried to make it clear they'd seen their stalwart compadre. All of a sudden, Marshal Court said, "What the hell's he doin'? Thought you told him to drop the dynamite on the cabin roof, Long."

"That's exactly what I told him. You stood right beside me when I said it."

"Well, he's makin' motions like he's up to somethin' else. Can't imagine what, but he's actin' mighty odd."

It took a bit, but Longarm finally figured out what Court's enthusiastic deputy had in mind. "Holy shit, boys. He's gonna blast that big ole rock up there loose and drop it right on top of Calico Jack's unsuspecting noggin."

Mike Rader made a sound like a pig snorting. "Bullshit. Rudy's a lot of things—brain smart ain't one of 'em. Most likely the poor goober'll blow his own dumbassed self clean to Kingdom Come."

Longarm snapped, "Get back to your shooting stations, gents. Let's give Calico Jack something to occupy his feeble thinker mechanism for a minute or so. Ain't no way we can stop Rudy from doin' whatever he has in mind now. So you fellers get to makin' some noise."

Soon as the rifle fire cranked up again, Rudy Crabtree disappeared from the precarious edge of the canyon wall like a puff of smoke. For some minutes, the booming sound of Winchesters drowned out just about any other noise a man might have made. Then a resounding thump, which shook the entire floor of Wild Horse Canyon, stopped all of the posse's concentrated blasting. Everyone backed away from his firing site, raised an anxious gaze, and stared awestruck at the events unfolding more than sixty feet above Calico Jack's stronghold.

At first, nothing extraordinary appeared to take place. Then a second rumbling thump rattled everyone's teeth, and the monstrous boulder began to slowly move forward and down. A wave of red dirt squirted from beneath the heavy stone and rained down on the cabin's poorly constructed roof like a heavenly shower of dirt, rubble, and crushed rock.

Longarm heard someone say, "Sweet Jesus. Looka that, would you? Fuckin' thing is huge. Bigger'n a Denver and Rio Grande locomotive."

Rudy Crabtree's third, and final, effort to move heaven and earth proved beyond any doubt that the boy must have had some powder monkey hidden somewhere deep inside. The explosion's concussive force hit everyone watching on the canyon floor directly in the face. From beneath the jagged stone, a prehistoric rumble welled up out of the earth's scarred and tortured hide. Slow and steady at first, the clap of doom grew, swelled, and turned into thunder.

All of a sudden, the boulder slipped free of its earthly bonds. The immense rock tipped forward as if a single grain of sand might stop it, then fell through the air like a gigantic rust-colored cannonball on its deadly way to an eternal resting spot below. It rocketed through Calico Jack's roof like a Comanche war spear. The rustic building exploded in a cyclone of flying wreckage.

Dust, wood splinters, and all manner of other debris shot toward heaven and in every direction imaginable. The front facade of the log shack splintered into a jillion fragmented chunks, as if all three sticks of dynamite had been detonated inside at the same time. Hand-hewn window frames, attached to the walls with wooden pegs, disintegrated and flew into pieces like shattered glass. The front door broke off its leather hinges, went spinning through the dust-choked air like a tin pie plate, and shot sixty feet down the hill toward the party of lawmen. Several lesser but equally damaging pieces of airborne, rocky debris followed their enormous leader from the canyon wall and crushed anything left standing below.

Longarm heeled it around the string of protective boulders for a closer look. The rest of the party followed as fast as they could run. Soon the entire group had assembled in an amazed knot of pointing, chin scratching, head shaking, and mumbled commentary.

Mike Rader gazed up at the mushroom-shaped cloud of thick, red dust hovering over the obliterated log structure and breathed, "Sweet Merciful Father. That's got to be the damnedest thing I've ever seen in my entire life. Watched a feller eat a live scorpion once in a travelin' show. Even had occasion to see Nekkid Nadine and her snake when I was in New Orleans. Hell, her trick with the serpent warn't nuthin' compared to this'un."

Stewart Potts yelped, "By God, fellers, think I'd pay hard coin to watch this here show again. Got any more of that dynamite, Marshal Long? Maybe we could set off another stick or three just for the pure fun of watchin' it go up."

Marshal Harley Court stared in wordless wonderment and, for several seconds, appeared overcome with astonishment.

Skunk Hornbuckle slipped up near Longarm's elbow. "Helluva performance you done put on for us today, Marshal Long. Hafta say I'm right glad I didn't rabbit on ya. Wouldna missed this dance for all the whiskey in Cheyenne. Bet folks'll be tellin' this tale for years to come and, by God, I was here to bear witness to the whole shebang. Christ, I ain't never even heard of nuthin' to match 'er."

Then, to everyone's slack-jawed bewilderment and total surprise, a singular and stunning miracle occurred. Calico Jack Blackman stumbled out of the billowing waves of dust churning their way down the hill. Like a ghostly performer in a traveling magician's show, the murderous outlaw wobbled into view. His hat and most of his clothing had gone missing. But somehow, in some astounding and unfathomable way, the man still had possession of a rifle. He rubber-legged a stumbling path down the slope like a man on a mission. Firing from the hip, the dynamite-and-boulder-blasted outlaw proceeded to spray a curtain of hot lead at anything that moved.

The second shot Blackman snapped off hit Skunk Hornbuckle smack between the eyes like a closed fist. The slug knocked the odiferous outlaw's head backward as if the angel of death had reached down from heaven and slapped him speechless.

Longarm glanced over just in time to see Skunk's dead muscles spasm in a useless effort to jerk the smelly killer back into an upright position. A stream of hot, purple blood spewed from the poor goober's shattered forehead in a stream the size of a grown man's finger and showered Longarm in the process. Then, Hornbuckle suddenly went as limp as a squeezed-out bartender's rag and dropped to the earth like a hundred-pound bag of bird shot.

Longarm, Marshal Court, and both of the astonished deputies came back to themselves like men brought out of a deep trance and proceeded to return fire as fast as they could lever shells through their rifles. But Calico Jack kept coming, and he laid down a relentless wall of air-splitting lead.

Jack's near-misses kicked dirt into Longarm's eyes, scared the hell out of the two Hadleyville deputies, and forced Longarm to spin on his heel and head back for cover behind one of the rocks. Before he could make it all the way to complete safety, a blue whistler from Blackman's amazingly accurate weapon burned a path above his ear and knocked him flat on his back.

The rest of the posse yelped and scattered like scared dogs. Marshal Court ran like hell, took a flying leap, and landed behind several stacked saddles piled near the campfire. He scrambled around on his belly, laid his weapon's barrel on a saddle for support, and took trembling aim.

Longarm swam back to the surface of his muddled senses, rose to one elbow, and fingered the bloody trench over his ear. Dizzy and tangle-headed, his bug-eyed gaze landed on the open muzzle of Calico Jack Blackman's still-smoking rifle. The killer grinned like a thing insane, took two steps that put him within spitting distance of his tormentor, then stopped and laughed out loud. He appeared mighty pleased with himself, and was happier than a gopher in soft dirt.

"Well, Marshal Custis 'By God' Long," the grinning outlaw spat, "you might wanna say a prayer, or two, maybe even three. Your immortal soul's in jeopardy, cocksucker. Way I've got this whole shootin' match figured, it's a good deal past your time to shake hands with Jesus, you law-bringin' son of a bitch."

Blackman flashed another cheery, yellow-toothed grin, then leveled the rifle up. He even took aim at Longarm's chest before Marshal Harley Court put one in the maniacal killer's fogged-up thinker box. The .45-caliber slug went in above Calico Jack's right eye and pushed most of his brains out the back of his thick skull.

Court's miraculous shot straightened Blackman up on the run-down heels of his worn-out boots. Surprised, fluttering eyes rolled up into their sockets. Then he went to ground like a sack full of dirty laundry and almost landed across Longarm's legs.

Court stormed up to Longarm's side and helped his bleeding counterpart scramble to his feet. For several seconds, both men stared down at the lifeless corpse. "Shit almighty," Court whispered, "he didn't even twitch."

Longarm pulled out a bandanna, pressed it to his wound, then turned and gazed at his savior in wonder. "You've never killed a man like this before, have you, Harley?"

Court appeared unable to move. "No, sir. I've shot

one or two in the service of my job, but I ain't never kilt none. Had hoped I'd never have to do such a horrible thing. But I sure as hell kilt this'un though."

Longarm slapped the unsettled Hadleyville lawman on the back. "Yes, indeed. You most certainly did, Harley. And you saved the hell out of my bacon in the process."

Chapter 4

In Denver, two weeks later, U.S. Marshal Billy Vail stared across the paper-littered top of his overburdened desk. A thick cloud of pungent cigar smoke hovered above his head. He gazed at Longarm through steepled fingers, nodded, then said, "That may well be the damnedest tale you've ever brought back from the field, Custis. My God, you've been party to some garter snappers in the past, but the oddity of the combined, bloody demise of Calico Jack and Skunk Hornbuckle will likely go down as one of the most amazing gun battles in the collective history of the West. Bet the papers back East have a field day with this one."

Slumped in Vail's guest chair and looking completely wrung out, Longarm snatched a well-chewed nickel cheroot from between chapped lips and shook it at his boss as though the cigar weighed fifty pounds. "Ah hell, Billy. Wasn't all that much to the dance. Not really. If you've seen one boulder the size of a boxcar fall off a cliff and destroy a house, hell, you've seen 'em all. Hornbuckle and Calico Jack gettin' dead in the process ain't nothin' more'n a bonus, far as I can tell."

"Come now, Custis. Cherry-cheeked Hadleyville deputy marshal dynamites a gigantic boulder onto the un-suspecting head of a desperado like Calico Jack. Then, ole Jack miraculously manages to survive the entire ex-plosive doo-dah, stumble down the hill, rifle in hand, and kill the blue-eyed hell out of Skunk Hornbuckle. Small-town marshal kills Calico Jack. Sounds like the kind of tale legends are made of to me."

"Christ's sake, Billy, legends?"

"People write ballads about shit like this, Custis. I can see it now, rinky-dink piano players in whorehouses all over the West will most likely be playing the 'Ballad of Wild Horse Canyon' 'fore we know it. Your name will be on the lips of every ivory tickler west of the Mis-sissippi."

"Yeah, well, Billy, here's the kicker to the whole deal: I've been out in the briars and the brambles for nigh on two months. Had to put up with a man—and I use the word *man* with great reluctance—who smelled like a week-dead stack of skunks for most of that time. Got myself shot. Even thought for a second or so that I'd never see the light of the Lord's next day again."

Longarm dropped the stub of his well-chewed che-root into the spittoon beside his chair. He pulled another and, with great ceremony, lit it, and blew smoke rings to-ward the ceiling, where they blended with the fragrant, gun metal–colored cloud already suspended there. He shook the fresh smoke at Vail. "Said all that, Billy, just so I could remind you that you've been a-promisin' me some time off for a coon's age. And I've decided that I'm gonna take some. At least two weeks, maybe even a bit more. Three or four weeks, if the feelin' suits me."

Vail's hands dropped to the arms of his overstuffed

Moroccan leather chair. "I think that's a fine idea, Custis. Nothing much going on right now that needs your immediate attention. Fact is, criminal activity in our jurisdiction appears to be on a downslope right this very minute. I'm of the opinion that some much-deserved rest and recreation is exactly the ticket."

"Rest and recreation. Now that sounds mighty sweet. As long as it involves liquor and women."

"What'd you have in mind for your time off, Custis?"

Longarm arched an eyebrow and cast a squinty-eyed look at his boss. "You're absolutely certain there ain't nothin' in the works that'll put the kibosh on me recreatin' in the company of bawdy women for a spell."

Vail's moonlike face broke into a wide smile. "Absolutely certain, Custis. Now, I must admit that events have changed some since yesterday afternoon. Otherwise, you'd be on a train headed for Las Cruces right this very minute."

Longarm groaned. He snatched his hat off and covered his face. His head fell back against the chair's thick, deep padding. Through the felt of his snuff-colored Stetson, he said, "Why'd you have me in mind for a trip to Las Cruces, Billy? What happened in that rat's nest?"

Vail sucked in a puff from his ax handle–sized cigar, then said, "Sure you want to know? Don't have to tell you, since the whole dance worked out to your distinct advantage."

Longarm jerked the hat away from his face, then dropped it in his lap. "Go on ahead and give me the whole weasel, Billy. Hell, I'm intrigued. Ain't every single day my luck holds long enough for something this good to happen."

Vail propped one foot on an open desk drawer and

pushed himself into a semi-reclined position. "Well, while you were down in Wild Horse Canyon, playin' with dynamite and laughing your ass off at Calico Jack's bizarre demise, an old friend of yours turned up in Las Cruces. Just thought you might like to slip on down that way and surprise him, that's all."

Through gritted teeth, Longarm snarled, "Get on with it, Billy. Which man-killin', woman-rapin', child-molestin', thievin' horse fucker turned up in Las Cruces? Please, please tell me before I just bust wide open from pent-up curiosity."

Vail tried to stifle a snorting laugh, but couldn't quite make the trick work. "Well, I'm sure you'll be happy to know that you've been denied an opportunity to kill the hell out of Shelby McMasters."

Longarm gagged, came nigh on spitting the fresh cheroot into his lap, leaned forward, and coughed like a man about to strangle slap to death. Eventually, he flopped back in his seat and stared into Marshal Billy Vail's grinning face. "Heard you say it, Billy, but I'm not sure what it all meant. Am I to take it as how that walkin' stack of hammered horse shit Shelby McMasters is now amongst the cold, cold dead?"

"You know me, Custis. Meant exactly what I said. Your old pal, a man who could chew off your plug anytime he wanted, bit the big one 'bout a week ago. His sad passing saved you a trip damned near to Mexico, that's for sure."

"Son of Satan ain't no friend of mine, and you goddamn well know it. Wouldn't let him touch my plug even if I'd just dropped it in the middle of a fresh pile of horse dung. Back-shootin' wretch put a hot, blue whistler in me down in the Guadalupe Mountains sev-

his feet. "Shit. Woulda give a month's pay to
hands on that skunk. You gonna tell me what
or do I have to go all the way to Las Cruce...

"Tragic story, Custis. Really tragic...
tears out of a glass eye. Gonna bre...
hear it. Kind of tale must ca...
misty eyed."

"Reckon I'll hear it'...
...by the secon...
roses. Way you...
for belly-scr...
Vail's...
pearan...
as...

that a... Shelby looked in
one o... curtly worded wire I received
informed me that he wanted me to send someone to es-
cort the prisoner to Denver for trial, and to be damned
quick about it."

"Sent me after him and Shelby might not've made it
to Denver alive."

"'Course, I wired back and informed Las Cruces's
head lawdog that I had just the man for the job—
meaning none other than you. Also mentioned that he'd
have to wait until you returned from your most recent
assignment. And, to finally answer your original question, yes, appears you missed your chance to kill Shelby
back in the Guadalupes, lo those many years ago, when
he shot you out of the saddle and left you to die."

Longarm hurled his dead cheroot into the spittoon at

37

... get my
... happened,
... es to find out?"
... Vale could squeeze
... k your heart when you
... use veteran angels to get

... fore I'm too old to care? Gettin'
... d, Billy. Agin' faster'n last spring's
... re a-goin' right now, I'll be in a home
... tchin' old idgits 'fore you get to tellin' it."
... smile grew more sinister. He took on the ap-
... ce of the cat that ate the canary. "Well, now, near
... ve been able to determine, from a number of exchanged telegrams, the story goes something like this.
Seems Shelby enjoyed the affections of a lewd woman.
Evidently, local constabulary made the mistake of al-
lowing her to visit him right regular in his cell. Postu-
lated theory, from the sheriff down that way, goes that
she must've agreed to smuggle a pistol into the outhouse
for him."

"Oh, that's original. Seems like I've heard somethin'
like that one before. Didn't that buck-toothed rodent
down Lincoln County way use that ruse once or twice?"

Vail ignored Longarm's reference to Henry McCarty
and kept hacking at his story. "Deputy in charge of the
jail walked ole Shelby out to do his business yesterday,
but from all indications, he couldn't find the secreted
weapon."

"What the hell does that mean—all indications?"

The grinning cat look spread over Vail's face again. He
leaned back in his seat and gazed at the ceiling as though
seeking divine guidance. "Well, ole Shelby must've been

38

leaning over into the shitter, feeling around under the seat, and somehow slipped."

Longarm's eyes widened. "Don't tell me. He fell in?"

"Head first."

"Sweet Jesus. Is that even possible?"

"Possible or not, that's exactly what appears to have happened. Deputy claims as how he didn't hear a thing."

"Lord Almighty."

"Can you imagine the thrashing around he must've done? Anyway, apparently McMasters got stuck."

"You don't mean it? Honest to God, the man went head first into the shitter?"

"Deputy finally went to rapping on the door after a prolonged silence of about ten or fifteen minutes. Had to break the door down to get in."

"And Shelby?"

Billy Vail slapped the top of his desk with an open palm and burst out laughing. "Drowned. Way I heard the tale, only part of 'im pokin' out of that two-holer were the soles of his boots."

Took a second or two, but the wonderfully rounded, cosmic beauty of the thing finally settled in. Longarm slapped his knee, bent over, and laughed till he hurt. Billy Vail joined in. Every time Longarm tried to get control of himself and sit up, another round of raucous guffaws hit both men.

Henry, Vail's concerned clerk, poked his head in the door, glanced around the room, and vanished as quickly as he'd appeared.

Through tears, Longarm moaned, "That's an elaborate joke, right, Billy? You're just kiddin'? McMasters is still alive and you just did this to put me in a good mood. That's the deal, ain't it?"

Vail wiped his eyes and held up his palm as though being sworn for court testimony. "God's truth, Custis. I swear it on my mother's sainted white head."

Longarm hopped out of his chair, slapped his hat on, and started for the door.

"Where you going, Custis?" Vail yelped at his deputy's back.

Longarm grabbed the knob to the U.S. marshal's office door and snatched it open. "Fort Worth," he said. "Siren call of Hell's Half Acre is ringing in my ears. A place where the women are willin' and the liquor flows like clear mountain streams. Right pleasant train ride this time of year. You have any need to get in touch with me, Billy, I'll be stayin' at the El Paso Hotel on Third Street."

"I know that hotel, Custis. One of the nicest in Fort Worth, if memory serves."

"Damn right. Fine lodgings are directly across the street from Luke Short's White Elephant Saloon. I intend to spend a good deal of my time playing poker, sampling fine rye whiskey, and making friends with any available female in that stellar establishment. Truth be told, though, I'd rather not hear from you, or your clerk, for a spell."

The door slammed shut. Marshal Billy Vail stared at it for a second, took another puff from his cigar, then watched another smoke ring float to the ceiling. He chuckled. "Enjoy yourself, Custis. You deserve it," he said to the empty office.

Chapter 5

Longarm stepped onto the loading platform of Union Depot in Fort Worth. A hot, dust- and grit-filled wind blew up from the south. He dropped his fully packed canvas travel bag on a convenient bench, then propped his ever-present Winchester and Greener atop the leather-strapped sack. The Denver, Texas, and Fort Worth Railroad's Baldwin engine idly chuffed and puffed on the track a few feet away. Amidst a billowing cloud of vented steam, Longarm twisted and stretched tight shoulders, stiff legs, and a kinked spine, all derived from long hours in the less-than-comfortable passenger car.

A molten sun, pasted to a near-cloudless sky, had begun to settle in the west when a graybeard with a slightly gimpy leg hobbled up, touched the brim of his tattered Confederate cavalry officer's hat, then said, "Hack, mister? Quarter'll git you to the center of town. Fifty cents an' I'll take you anyplace you wanna go. Dollar and I'm yours for the entire afternoon."

"Can you make more than one stop?"

"Sure thang. Till I deliver you to your final destination, my time is yers." A fist-sized wad of tobacco bulged in the

41

man's cheek. Juice leaked from the corners of a toothless mouth and stained his ragged chin hair.

Longram nodded, then attempted to carry his grip to the unkempt gent's flatbed spring wagon. But the limping driver wouldn't allow it. He shook his head, then eased the burden from Longarm's grasp.

"My pleasure, sir. Also my livin'. You take the rifle. Never attempt to handle other men's weapons, lest they disapprove. But I'll get the bag," he said, and smiled.

Three blocks from the train station, a tired gray mare pulled the well-used wagon up Main Street past a joint called the Local Option Saloon. Swarms of people swept up and down the rutted dirt thoroughfare like waves on a rocky beach. Cowhands, gamblers, drummers, drunks, whores, pimps, and evangelizing Bible-thumpers, people of every kind, size, and stripe milled about in a seething mass of constantly moving humanity.

The hack driver nodded toward the Local Option's coarse edifice, then said, "We kin stop, if'n you've a need fer a drink. Built this place as close to the depot as they could, jus' fer the convenience of travelin' folk. Feller what slings the booze inside actually has cold beer fer a nickel a glass. Right fine stuff on a day like this'un."

Longarm glanced at the cow-country cantina's broad false front. A brightly painted sign over the batwing doors proclaimed it the place where you could get the "worst liquor, poorest cigars, and most miserable pool tables" in Fort Worth. Hordes of noisy customers seethed in and out of the crowded doorway. He chuckled, then said, "Think I'll pass on that one, friend. Let's head on up toward the center of town, maybe it ain't so busy."

The driver grinned. "Got several big trail herds bedded down on the north side of the Trinity. Pretty much every grog shop in town's swamped right now. You gonna be stickin' around long, mister?"

"Week, maybe two, if things work out the way I hope they do."

"Be needin' a nice place to stay then, I'd imagine."

"My sentiments exactly."

"El Paso Hotel's right fine. Caters to a better'n average clientele. Mosta these cowboys sleep with their herds. Cain't afford rooms in a swanky joint like the El Paso."

"Must be some kind of mind reader, my friend. That's the very spot I'd decided on before stepping off the train."

"You gotta reservation?"

"Reservation? No, don't have a reservation."

"Well, if'n you'll allow it, when we arrive, let me tell the desk clerk I directed you to the place."

Longarm hesitated, then said, "They pay you a bit for sendin' customers their way?"

"Yessir. They do at that. Ain't much, but everythang I can scratch up helps."

"Fine by me."

"Thanky, sir. Name's Willard Allred. Formerly of Lowndes County, Alabama."

"My pleasure, Mr. Allred."

"You can call me Tater. Most everybody else does."

"Tater?"

"Yep. See, durin' Mr. Lincoln's War of Yankee Aggression again' the South, spent a good deal of the unpleasantness locked up in one of his nightmarish prisons for captive cavalry officers. Lived on taters for nigh on eighteen months. Them as survived with me started a-callin' me Tater. Unfortunately, the name stuck."

"Tater might be a stretch for me, friend. But I'll try

'er ever' once in a while. Custis Long here. My distinct pleasure to make your acquaintance."

"Pleasure's all mine, sir. So, it's the El Paso we're a-wantin' to head fer, Mr. Long?"

"Well, not just yet. First, let's make a stop at the city marshal's office, Tater. Think it best I check in with local law enforcement. Usually a good idea when I'm in town."

Tater Allred swiveled his deeply creased, stubble-covered face around and considered his passenger with a spark of renewed interest. He studied Longarm for several seconds, then turned back to his driving. "You a law bringer, Custis? Suffer under the man-killin' weight of a tin star?"

"Deputy U.S. marshal. Based outta the Federal District Court in Denver. But I'm not here on official business this time around. Takin' me a brief respite from the rigors of chasin' bad men and bad women into bad places."

"Picked about as good a town as any in Texas fer recreatin'. Acre gets a-goin' like a steam calliope in a travelin' carnival, soon's the sun goes down."

"You mean this crowd is just typical run of the mill for an average afternoon these days?"

"Yep. Place'll git right busy in two, maybe three hours."

"Well, she's changed a bit since my last visit. Seems to me like Long Haired Jim Courtright was still ramrod-ing the law around these parts when last I passed this way. 'Course my questionable recollection could suffer some. Wouldn't be the first time."

Allred cut loose with a massive gob of tobacco juice, hocked into the dusty street, just as they passed in front

44

of the Emerald Saloon. The crowd appeared not to have diminished by a single person. "Ole Long Hair enjoyed the affection and goodwill of nigh on the whole county, till he went and took to the bottle. Got ta actin' right peculiar toward the end of his last term. Made some mighty poor decisions. Never did seem too interested in actually enforcin' the law to start with. But then, he fell into drunkenness, bad behavior, and poorly considered acts of outright extortion, there at the end."

"I'd heard the good citizens here'bouts had voted him out."

"Yep. Feller name of Sam Farmer's in charge of the Fort Worth police force now."

"What's Farmer like?"

"Bit more energetic at enforcin' city ordinances, I suppose. But to tell you the God's truth, Custis, he ain't much better'n the average town marshal you'd meet up with in any small Texas town. Some like him, some don't. Most of the Acre liked Long Haired Jim better, mainly 'cause he turned a blind eye to damn near anythang they chose to do."

All along Main, on either side of the street, Longarm took note of thriving, busy parlor houses that appeared to have sprouted like Texas wildflowers. Peppered here and there, crib shacks and rough-looking dance halls popped up—usually as near to a convenient saloon as possible.

Wagon yards, mule barns, and stables were mixed in here and there. But the jam-packed, cheek-by-jowl building methods of most cities and towns didn't appear to apply to Fort Worth. Watering holes, dance halls, and sporting establishments were scattered along the streets, and large, open, unfilled gaps between them appeared fairly typical. Such construction methods gave the town that wide-open feel so often described in the penny dreadfuls so popular back East.

Most of the coarse-built structures they passed appeared not to have been in place for any length of time. The board-and-batten shacks were predominately constructed from rough-cut, unseasoned lumber that still oozed thick streams of gooey sap. And while the false fronts of every liquor locker and cantina sported garish paint jobs, few, if any, of the sporting houses, and none of the cribs, had yet been graced with the loving touch of a painter's brush.

Shameless women hawked their carnal wares from doorways and windows, and some walked boldly up and down the street in various states of dress and undress. A hard-eyed gal with hair the color of flame staggered along beside Longarm's hack and plucked at his sleeve. Wearing nothing more than open-crotched pantalets and a chemise that did nothing to cover her melon-sized breasts and dark nipples, she grabbed his hand and placed it on one of her swaying tits.

"Wanna ride the tiger, mister?" she yelled. "Jus' get your stringy ass down outta that wagon, big boy. You can fuck me right here in the street. Do the deed in the bed of your wagon. Won't cost but a dollar. A damned fine deal. I'm juicier'n a ripe melon. Jus' waitin' fer you to make up your mind. I get done and you'll swear you just fucked a Comanche squaw whose ass was on fire. Ask your driver, he knows me."

"Git the hell away, Iris," Allred snapped. "This gent don't need nothin' you're a-sellin'."

In a halfhearted attempt to remain the gracious

Southern gentleman, Longarm tipped his hat and said, "No thanks, miss. Perhaps at some later time."

"How 'bout a nice blow job. Suck you till your head caves and your spurs start spinnin' like a Fourth of July whizbang. Do you for fifty cents. Ain't no other woman in Hell's Half Acre can suck your dick like me. I can lick the leather cover off a saddle horn."

Longarm jerked his sleeve out of the unrelenting woman's grip. "Appreciate the offer, miss, but think I'll pass."

Iris stopped dead in her tracks. She grabbed up a wad of something at her feet and threw it. The pile shattered against the spring wagon's side boards. "Well, then, you can go straight to hell, you penny-pinchin' son of a bitch," she screeched. "Girl's gotta make a livin', for Christ's sake. Guess you figure I ain't good enough. High-toned bastard. Wouldn't suck your dick now for a hundred dollars, by God."

Over his shoulder, Longarm glanced back at the angry girl. "Testy little thing, ain't she, Tater?"

"Yeah, they's a lot of 'em jes' like 'er workin' the streets. Rough ole gals. Most of 'em ain't seen twenty yet, but they're tougher'n a chewed boot heel. Come out here straight off Louisiana farms and Texas ranches. All of 'em young, big-eyed, mostly innocent, and lookin' fer adventure. Year or so sellin' themselves, and even the sweetest little country girl ever born gets harder'n a chunk of flint."

"What're the borders of Hell's Half Acre these days, Tater?"

"Oh, from about Ninth Street south to the depot, and everything from Throckmorton on the west to Calhoun,

47

or maybe Jones, on the east. Most everythang from about Fifth Street north is considered the better part of town. That's where the El Paso and the White Elephant are located."

At Main and Fourth Street, Allred used his whip to point out the Mansion House Hotel, but immediately qualified his praise by saying, "But if'n I had the money, I'd stick with your original choice, Custis. El Paso's closer to Luke Short's White Elephant, and that's as nice a gamblin' and eatin' joint as you'll find in the entire West. Jus' a few steps 'cross Third Street and you're right at the front door."

"I met Luke Short in Tombstone not long after he snuffed Charlie Storms's lamp. And we've run into one another a time or two since. 'Bout as nice a feller as you'd like to meet, as long as you don't piss him off."

"Wouldn't know anythang 'bout that myself, but yours appears to be the prevailin' opinion on the subject. Lookin' the raggedy-assed way I do, ain't never had nerve enough to go inside the place. Stood at the door a time or two, though. Took a gander at the wonders they offer. Swanky stuff fer a frontier burg like Fort Worth. But that's jes' my opinion, and the opinions of fellers like me don' mean much."

The farther north they traveled along Main Street, the cleaner and more pretentious the town became. Parlor houses, cribs, stables, wagon yards, and dance halls gave way to fancy eating establishments, like the Merchant's Restaurant, several theaters, and a number of classy hotels. In the distance, the street came to a dead end directly in front of the imposing, still new, but somewhat strange-looking Tarrant County Courthouse. Laid out somewhat like the spokes around the center hub of a wheel, the building was unlike any Longarm had ever seen before.

Allred eased his rickety wagon past the El Paso Hotel, the White Elephant, and Theatre Comique, turned right on Second Street, then headed for the city jail. He reined to a stop at the corner of Second and Rusk. In appearance, the coarse city marshal's office and jail didn't look all that different from the shabby cribs they'd passed along the way—it was simply a good bit larger and decorated with heavy iron bars on the windows and doors.

Longarm climbed down from Tater Allred's wagon, slipped a silver dollar into the old soldier's trembling hand, told him to wait, then hopped up on the jail's porch and pushed his way inside without knocking. Once over the threshold, he closed the door and hesitated long enough to allow his eyes to adjust to the room's darker interior.

Several hard-looking men, dressed in a kind of rudimentary uniform that consisted of knee-length gray coats, black slouch hats, and large official-looking six-pointed stars lounged around a desk in one corner of the room. Gun racks laden with a variety of weapons, ammunition, leg irons, and other methods of restraint covered the north wall of the cramped space. A tin stove, rough table, and handmade checkerboard in the corner opposite the marshal's desk were surrounded by a mixed collection of mismatched chairs, stools, and empty, upturned wooden shipping crates.

Barred doors across the entire back wall of Fort Worth's jailhouse led the way into a cellblock that appeared fully capable of housing several hundred prisoners. An odor, rank enough to curl a man's nose hair, oozed from the empty-appearing calaboose like an invisible cloud of stink from a cattle pen.

A florid-faced, black-haired gent seated behind the desk sported a waxed handlebar moustache the size of a man's forearm. On his chest, the distinctive gold badge of the city marshal twinkled in the room's sparse light.

The marshal motioned Longarm forward and said, "Come right on in, sir. These fellers are on their way out. Job of keepin' a lid on things around here ain't never done."

One of the policemen grunted, rose from the only other available chair near the desk, touched the brim of his hat, and headed for the door. His fellow officers followed. In pretty short order, Longarm and Fort Worth's chief law enforcement officer had the entire dank-smelling room to themselves.

Sam Farmer motioned for his guest to sit, offered up a politician's painted-on smile, then said, "How can the Fort Worth city police be of assistance today?"

Longarm removed his hat, yanked a bandanna from his pocket, and wiped his sweaty head and face. Then he pulled his wallet from an inside jacket pocket and flipped it open to reveal his deputy U.S. marshal's badge and official credentials. "Name's Custis Long, Marshal Farmer. In town for a few days of rest and recreation. Nothing official, mind you. Just stopped by to let you know I'm in town."

Farmer's gaze darted from the badge to Longarm's face, then back again. He leaned forward in the squeaky chair and placed his elbows on the desk. He peaked his fingers, then rested his chin against his thumbs, as if in deep contemplation. "Most gracious of you to come in for a visit today, Marshal Long," he said. "Want you to know I do appreciate the thoughtfulness of the courtesy you've so graciously extended."

"Well, Marshal, I've always made it my practice to keep in close touch with local constabulary, no matter my business. Hope you understand and approve."

"Oh, I do, Marshal Long. Indeed, sir. Must admit that, when I took office, I made the mistake of letting personal fears and political resentment color my attitudes toward other members of the law enforcement fraternity. But I've adjusted that faulty attitude considerably over the past year or so. Do make yourself at home while visiting my town, and feel free to call on me for anything you might need. I'll be most pleased to assist in any way I can."

Longarm stuffed his hat back on, then stood. "Well, do appreciate your offer, sir. Right now I'd like to head for the hotel and get settled." He extended a hand.

Farmer kept his seat, but shook his guest's hand, then, as Longarm headed for the door, he said, "Hope we can have a drink while you're in town, Marshal Long."

Standing on the threshold, with the brass knob in hand, Longarm turned, then touched the brim of his hat. "I look forward to that pleasant instance and would be most happy to stand you to a beaker of your favorite poison at your own convenience. You can find me at the El Paso Hotel, Marshal, or just get in contact with my driver, Mr. Allred. We've come to an arrangement, and he'll always be aware of where I am as long as I'm in town."

Chapter 6

Limping as though he could barely make it, Willard Allred lugged Longarm's canvas bag up to the imposing three-story brick El Paso Hotel's solid walnut check-in desk and dropped it on the floor.

Longarm glanced around the enormous lobby and noted that it looked more like a European opera house than a Texas hotel. All the furnishings appeared new and impressively expensive. Well-dressed men, of obvious substance, sat at small tables placed around the open vestibule. They read newspapers, smoked their ax handle–sized cigars, or talked with one another in hushed tones behind cupped palms.

Underfoot, a meticulously clean, thick, dark-colored Brussels carpet deadened the building's interior noise and added a peaceful, relaxing feel to the place. A staircase nearby led to the two upper floors, and across the foyer a set of highly polished batwings opened into a convenient saloon and billiards room. Another entryway, gilt decorated and gleaming, led into the hotel's private dining area. A beautiful young woman manned a desk beside the door. Might have to spend some time in both those places, Longarm thought, then smiled at the prospect of the entertainment possibilities afforded by such an onsite convenience.

A slick-haired, clean-shaven, imperially slim clerk, dressed in a suit and spotless white shirt that made a man want to cover his eyes, hustled over, nodded, then said, "Who do we have with us today, Tater?"

"Custis Long, deputy U.S. marshal outta Denver, Mr. Hunter. He'd like a room with a bath for a week, maybe two."

Hunter sniffed, then twirled the thick, leather-bound registration book around on its swiveling stand. "Please sign here, Mr. Long. I'm sure the El Paso can accommodate your every need and desire during your stay."

Longarm took up the pen, dipped it, then signed his name. He laid the pen aside, then said, "Well, Mr. Hunter, what I need right now is a bath and one of your valets to take my suit to a laundry. Have it brushed and pressed. What I might desire later could prove problematic. But we'll hold off on that for the present."

Allred waved a uniformed hotel employee aside and insisted on carrying the heavy bag all the way to Longarm's room. He knew exactly where to go as soon as the room number came from the desk clerk's mouth, and led the way as though the sumptuous lodgings were his own.

He ushered Longram around the elegantly appointed room, bragged about the help, the in-house bar, the billiards room, and the restaurant, then doffed his hat and headed for the door. "Been my pleasure, Marshal Long. Hope you enjoy your stay. And, oh, thanks for allowin' me to pull one over on Mr. Hunter. Hotel pays me two dollars for every guest I appear to guide their direction."

Longarm gazed at the bed, polished walnut furnishings, metal bath in the corner, and back to Allred. "Tell me, Tater, how much do you make on an average day a-haulin' folks back and forth from the depot?"

Allred scratched his chin. "Oh, at twenty-five cents a trip, best I ever done was four dollars. But that were durin' the busiest part of the cattle season. 'Course, if'n I can git a feller like you, the El Paso's added income fer bringin' you in helps considerable. Guess you could say three to four dollars in a day's a damn good'un. But I've been known to take a siesta, here and there. Rarely work all day at a single spurt."

"Here's what I'll do. You make yourself available for me, kind of semi-exclusively, while I'm in town, and I'll give you ten dollars cash money right now, and ten more the day you take me to the depot when I leave. All you have to do is check in with the desk two or three times a day to find out if I need you."

Allred's rheumy eyes lit up. "Damn, didn't realize lawmen made that kinda money. Ever' one of 'em as I've knowed was poor as church mice."

Longarm waved the old soldier's concern away. "Well, I've been savin' for more years than I care to remember for this trip. Money is not a problem. There's plenty. Trust me when I say I've not had an opportunity to spend much of my salary for some years now. Stuff's just been sittin' in a bank in Denver, gatherin' interest."

"I see."

"Does my proposition have any appeal for you?"

Allred stuffed his hat on, came to military attention, and saluted. "Mr. Long, you've got yourself a private guide to all the wonders, carnal and otherwise, of Fort Worth in general and Hell's Half Acre in particular. You just tell me what you're lookin' for, or what you want, and by God, we'll find it. If'n Tater Allred cain't find it, then a man sure as hell don't need it."

Longarm placed the ten-dollar gold piece in Allred's palsied hand, then clapped the man on the back. "Pick yourself a spot in the shade and take a load off for a spell. Soon's I get cleaned up, we'll get out amongst 'em and see what we can get into."

Allred rolled the coin around in his fingers, then stuffed it into the pocket of his raggedy vest. "Be waitin' fer you. Don't worry, I'll spot you soon's you hit the street again, Mr. Long."

"I'd feel a lot more comfortable if you called me Custis, Tater."

"See you downstairs—Custis."

Two hours later, Longarm, bathed and shaved, stepped onto the El Paso Hotel's covered veranda. He stopped a moment, then lit a fresh cheroot. His brown tweed suit, snuff-colored Stetson, and low-heeled boots had all been brushed, and the suit carefully pressed. As he ran a finger back and forth under his heavy moustache, he watched Willard Allred hobble across Third Street from the direction of the White Elephant.

"Been starin' in the door again like a kid at the candy counter?"

"Yeah. Gonna work up nerve enough to stroll in one a these days."

"Hell, you don't have any problem strollin' into the nicest hotel in town. Why does a saloon slow you down?"

Allred tilted his head like a confused hound. "Not sure, exactly. It's just different, that's all. Hell, I've got an accommodation with these folks here at the El Paso.

Ain't managed to get nothin' goin' over at the White Elephant. Besides, a man kinda feels obligated to spend money in a place like the Elephant. Money I ain't always got to throw around."

Longarm glanced up and down the darkening thoroughfare. Both Main and Third Streets teemed with bustling knots of laughing, loud-talking people. Men and women strolled arm in arm. Cowboys, freighters, gamblers, and travelers of every imaginable stripe moved about between large puddles of flickering light created by lamps behind the opaque windows of various businesses along the streets.

Allred tilted his head back and sniffed the air. "Do I detect the hint of toilet water waftin' off a your person, Custis?"

Longarm snatched the cheroot from between his lips and smiled. "Women tend to like a man who smells like something other'n sweat, dirt, a nasty ass, and horses, Tater. And when it comes to women, I'm gonna do whatever it takes to make 'em happy."

"Ah. Well, of the worldly pleasures available to a man down in the Acre, am I to assume that women are the first order of business this evenin'?"

The cheroot traveled from one corner of Longarm's mouth to the other. "Perhaps a bit later in the evening. We'll just have to wait and see what kind of opportunity presents itself. Right now, I could use a good meal, two or three glasses of good Maryland rye, and maybe a bit of poker to top off my first evening in town."

"Fine eatin' joint right here in the hotel. Mighty good'un in the Elephant, too. Merchant's Restaurant over yonder across Main's a favorite spot for visitin' cattlemen. Any of 'em are good. Just take your pick."

Longarm turned, clapped Allred on the shoulder, then said, "Come along, Willard. I'll treat you to a beaker of your favorite spirits at the White Elephant. Then you can head home for a much-deserved night's rest. Figure I'm not gonna be needin' your services tonight."

Yellow-tinted lamplight, laughter, and music poured from behind the White Elephant's inviting doors. Allred followed Longarm inside, but hesitated once he'd crossed the threshold, and appeared reluctant to go any farther. For a second, the poor man seemed unable to believe the beauty of what presented itself for his unfettered examination.

A few steps over the Elephant's threshold, a wide, carpeted staircase led to the second floor gaming area. The clicking sounds made by a roulette wheel and a Keno game's goose filtered down the steps like cascading water and invited the potential risk taker to come on up and put his money on the line. To the right of the flight of steps, the famed saloon's restaurant beckoned, and on the left, the most famous bar in the entire West loomed, in all of its mirrored splendor.

Tater Allred gazed up to the landing at the top of the carpeted stairway and, in a voice filled with pious awe, said, "Done heard tell they's a table up yonder what has fifty thousand dollars in gold coin stacked on it fer anyone as passes to stop and gaze on. Can you imagine— fifty thousand dollars in gold, Marshal Long? Must be an amazin' sight."

Longarm swept an all-encompassing arm around the saloon's grandiose entry, then pointed at the bar. "Forget the gold—take a long, lovin' look at that, Willard. Ain't that the most beautiful thing you've ever seen?

Sweet Jesus, she must be damned near fifty feet of polished mahogany and twinklin' glass. My oh my, take a gander at all the liquor on the back bar. Splendid, ain't it? Just damned splendid."

Allred removed his hat as though he'd just entered the sanctuary of a stone cathedral inhabited by the twin gods of drink and chance. He twisted the battered head cover in his hands and moaned like a man in the throes of malarial agony. "You sure about this, Marshal Long? Okay that I'm here?"

Longarm took the old cavalry officer by the elbow and ushered him to a spot at the establishment's magnificent, gleaming bar. He made a flicking motion at a slick-headed, smiling drink slinger, who quickly hustled over and wiped a spot off for them.

Longarm turned to Tater and said, "What'll you have, Mr. Allred. Pick anything they've got. It's on me."

Allred's withered, scar-covered hand came up to the bar's surface and caressed the polished wood as though it were a living thing. Longarm barely heard the man when he said, "Kentucky bourbon and branch water, Custis. A double, if that's alright."

A broad smile etched its way across Longarm's face. "You heard the gentleman, barkeep. And you can bring me a double shot of your best Maryland rye."

When the liquor arrived, Longarm held his glass aloft, then said, "Let's see if I can remember a toast, Willard. Ah, yeah, bet this'un will work just fine: Here's to the man who makes me laugh; who makes me forget my sorrow. May he have a big, fat bank account, and friends who never borrow."

A flush-faced Allred offered up a gap-toothed smile, tapped his glass against that of his newly found friend, then took a nibbling sip. He ran his tongue across chapped lips. "Damn. Compared to what I usually drink, that's mighty fine giggle juice, Marshal Long," he said, then nibbled at the liquid fire again.

Barely a minute after their drinks hit the bar, a handsome young woman dressed in a wine-colored evening gown touched Longarm's elbow. Brown, almost black, eyes danced with promise when her gaze drank him in from head to foot. In a voice that sounded like a ten-pound cat purring, she said, "Would you like to have dinner with us tonight, sir? The White Elephant has one of the finest dining rooms in all of Texas."

Longarm flashed the girl a winning smile, then touched the brim of his hat. "That we would, my dear. My friend and I are hungry enough to eat the blades off a West Texas windmill. So, you just go on ahead and lead us to a proper table and bring on the beefsteak."

Allred refused to move from his spot. "You go on ahead, Marshal. Now that I've finally made it to Luke Short's magnificent drinkin' emporium, think I'd like to stay here at the bar for a spell. Kinda soak it all in for a bit, so to speak. Perhaps even have another glass of this fine tonsil paint, 'fore I trundle my way home for the evenin'."

Longarm glanced back and forth from Allred to the stunning young woman a time or two, then said, "Well, I've never been one to force food on anybody. But if you change your mind, Willard, just have this lovely lady bring you on back. Sure she can find a place for you to sit."

"I will, sir. I will."

Longarm took his drink and followed his beautiful guide. He'd taken only two or three steps before he stopped when Allred said, "Damned nice of you to bring me in here. Won't forget this, Marshal Long. No sir, won't forget it for quite a spell. Ain't many men who've bothered to treat me as well as you have this afternoon and this evenin'."

"My distinct pleasure, Tater." Longarm glanced over at the bartender again. "Give this gentleman anything he wants, barkeep. Just add it to my bill in the restaurant."

In the White Elephant's sumptuously appointed ground-floor eatery, Longarm took a brocaded seat at a corner table, next to a window that looked onto Fort Worth's main thoroughfare. The street now glittered and glowed in the soft lamplight that poured from doorways and other windows like yellow-tinted waterfalls at the ends of strange, dark rivers.

He scanned through a bill of fare that included "the best beefsteak in Texas, fresh fish, oysters, and game of all kinds." The meal that came to his table that night included a sampling of almost everything available. And after nigh on two hours of overindulgence, he slapped his full stomach, felt gloriously satisfied, pleased with his choices, and more relaxed than he'd been in months. He slid down in his chair and closed his eyes for a second. Heaven, he thought. Absolute heaven. But then an argument at a nearby table bubbled up, got violent, and snatched him out of his pleasant reveries.

Chapter 7

Longarm had noticed the woman sitting nearby within seconds of taking his own seat. Auburn-haired, petite, dark-eyed, ruby-lipped, and dressed in a high-necked, dove-gray dress with white ruffles at the throat, she was the kind any man would have easily described as a rare beauty. Dramatically striking and stately, he immediately recognized her as a distinct anomaly in most of the West, where life tended to be relentlessly hard on everyone, but destructive in the extreme when it came to the fairer sex. But more important than all of that, he took note of how she occasionally cast nervous, fleeting glances his way and, sometimes, appeared to allow herself a partial, tense smile when doing so.

All Longarm could see of the lady's combative companion, who was mostly hidden behind the glossy green leaves of a large potted plant, was a portion of the man's wide back and a flushed ear that peeked from a pile of stringy shoulder-length hair. But he didn't miss the snakelike arm that flicked out, or the broad, hard hand that smacked the woman across the mouth and drew blood to already crimson lips.

Appearing shocked and embarrassed by the vicious turn of events, the brown-eyed beauty ducked her head and tried to hide the consequences of the blow. Longarm grimaced. Nothing worse than being slapped in public, he thought, then took another sip from his recently refilled glass. That's the exact kind of stupidity that could get a man killed if he tried it on the wrong person.

The second lick sounded like a pistol shot and snapped Longarm's head back, as though he'd taken the forceful blow himself. He grunted like a teased circus bear on a thick metal chain, stood, then dropped a twenty-dollar gold piece on the table to cover the meal. He took his time and downed the last swallow from the fresh double shot of Maryland rye, slid the empty glass onto the littered table, then strode to the lady's side.

Tears streaked her reddened cheeks. Longarm could see the imprint of the hand on her face—each and every thick, stubby finger had left a mark. She glanced up at him as though pleading for help, but quickly let her gaze drop to the hands in her lap, where she absentmindedly twisted at a rouge-stained napkin.

Longarm stopped, tipped his hat in the woman's direction, then glanced down at the brute who'd twice slapped the hell out of the lady in a busy, popular restaurant filled with people. Square-jawed, beady-eyed, and obviously drunk, the woman's assailant snapped, "What the fuck you want, asshole?"

Longarm bowed slightly at the waist. "Couldn't help but notice this beautiful young woman's unnecessary distress. Thought perhaps I might be of some assistance."

The bruiser leaned back in his chair. He hooked his

thumbs into the pockets of his vest, then said, "I don't need no assistance from you, or any other cocksucker in this goddamn dump. So why don't you jus' shut the fuck up and hike your long, stringy ass on back to wherever'n hell you came from, 'fore I get up out'n this here chair and kick the shit outta you."

"Bold talk from a man sittin' down, who's gonna have to get to his feet before I beat the hell out of him."

The bruiser snarled, like a cornered cur. His lip peeled back over yellowed, canine teeth. "Well, then, don't do somethin' stupid enough to make me get up. If'n I have to get outta my seat, I'm gonna bust you out like a kid's paper bag full of horehound candy. Damn sure ain't gonna sit here much longer and listen to your kinda lip."

Longarm smiled. He snapped a quick, concerned glance at the teary-eyed woman. "Do hope you'll pardon me, ma'am. This won't take but a moment."

The Colt Frontier model pistol resting in Longarm's cross-draw holster flashed out. Its heavy barrel caught the drunken bully flush across the skull a few inches above the bridge of his nose. A pink spray of flying blood splattered the greenery sitting nearby.

The carefully applied blow knocked the thug backward nigh two feet. His chair legs squawked in protest on the polished hardwood floor. The wobbling seat went over and dumped the abusive bully on his back in a semiconscious, twitching heap. A deep gash sliced across the brute's rock-hard noggin, flowed freely, and leaked a wide pool of blood onto the floor beneath him. He pissed himself, then threw up.

The hostess in the wine-colored dress, a waiter who appeared on the edge of apoplexy, and a muscular, thick-necked bouncer arrived at the table at almost the same instant. Longarm slid the long-barreled pistol back into its holster and raised his hands in a gesture of reassurance.

"No need to be concerned, folks," he said. "Nothing to worry yourselves about. I'll gladly pay to have the floor and wall cleaned, but would like to suggest you remove this heap of woman-abusing trash from my sight before I completely lose any control of my temper I have left and stomp the absolute livin' hell out of 'im."

An elegantly dressed gentleman, whom Longarm immediately recognized, pushed his way through the growing crowd. His snow-white shirt, tailored suit, diamond stickpin, and highly buffed boots advertised his chosen profession as a sporting man. The bulge in a pants pocket Longarm knew to be leather lined gave away the presence of a heavy pistol. His diminutive stature ensured that even the least-informed visitor in all of Fort Worth would have recognized the White Elephant's colorful, and dangerous, owner—Luke Short.

Short's face broke into a wide, moustachioed smile, and he extended his hand. "Well, I'll just be damned. If it ain't the one and only Deputy U.S. Marshal Custis Long."

Longarm shook Short's immaculately clean, manicured paw, slapped the pocket-sized gambler on the shoulder, then said, "Been a spell, ain't it, Luke?"

"Well, yes it has. Two, maybe even three years, I'd venture. Silver City, I think."

"Coulda been. Yessir, coulda been."

Short glanced at the unconscious drunk lying on the floor of his restaurant in a puddle of piss, puke, and blood. "Hit him pretty hard, didn't you, Custis?"

"Well, he's a big ole boy. Big enough that I figured it best not to let him get outta his chair, if possible. But, gotta tell you, my pistol bounced right off his thick head like I'd whacked an oak stump."

Short reclaimed his hand, stepped over to a bloodless spot beside the man on the floor, then said, "Looks like you knocked him colder than a log-splitting wedge in Montana, Custis. What'd he do to piss you off?"

Longarm motioned toward the woman. "Son of a bitch slapped the hell outta this lady. Mighta been able to forgive such stupidity once. But hell, he did it twice. Don't know 'bout anyone else, but I can't abide a man who'll abuse a woman like that."

Luke Short shot a bored, somewhat less-than-interested glance at the damaged lady. "Just can't get away from those Southern-bred cavalier's ways, can you, Custis? Always out to help defenseless women, old people, and children. As I'm a bettin' man, I'd bet that some skirt-wearing twitch is gonna get you killed one of these days."

"You know me, Luke. Have a right tender spot in my heart for the weaker sex. 'Specially when they have to defend themselves from the likes of that blockheaded, thick-skulled bastard."

Short took Longarm by the elbow. In a low and conspiratorial voice, he said, "Might wanta get her outta here, Custis. We'll take care of her companion. I'll have my bouncers drag him out into the alley, drop him in a nice pile of garbage, and let him sleep off that rap across the face you gave him. Maybe he'll learn something from this experience, but I doubt it. Men like this one aren't usually all that bright, and it's been my experience that most are the kind who'll carry a grudge around for a lifetime." Short paused for a second, glanced down at the prostrate man again, then said, "Probably should have just gone ahead and killed him."

Longarm nodded. "Well, just couldn't bring myself to impose on your hospitality like that, Luke." Then he swung back around to the table and held out his hand. The shattered woman dabbed at her eyes with a tiny handkerchief. "Think it's best if you'd come with me, ma'am. We'll take the air along Main Street for a few minutes. Give you a chance to clear your head. No need to stay here any longer."

As she rose, her trembling hand grasped his arm. He led her to the White Elephant's door, and from there onto the boardwalk along Fort Worth's busy Main Street. The broiling heat of the day had abated a bit with the setting of a molten sun. A breeze out of the north that felt almost cool stirred the dense, dusty air.

The seething crowd on the boardwalk and in the streets and doorways appeared to have grown dramatically during Longarm's meal in the White Elephant's fancy restaurant. Gas lamps flickered atop iron poles on almost every corner, but offered little in the way of real illumination.

The muffled popping of gunshots—from a busy shooting gallery named Blackwell's located right next door to Luke Short's sumptuous palace of earthly delights—sounded like the dampened explosions of fancy Chinese fireworks on the occasion of a festive celebration, or perhaps an election. Spent gunpowder laced the night air with an acrid smell that passersby could easily taste.

Knots of exuberant cowboys, dressed in colorful bandannas and massive Boss of the Plains hats, jingled up and down both sides of the street in search of liquor, women, and entertainment. Horses crowded the hitch rails, switching their tails and stamping their feet to shoo enormous flies away. The carefree sounds of laughter and rinky-dink piano music rose and fell with the opening and closing of every door.

Longarm guided his beautiful charge across the dusty thoroughfare, then stopped on the walkway in front of Merchant's Restaurant long enough for her to cling to his arms, lean against his chest, and weep.

As tenderly as possible, Longarm used his finger to lift the weeping woman's face so he could gaze into her eyes. Flickering lamplight played across the flawless skin of her face and heightened an already stunning beauty. When she leaned against him, her head hit him in the middle of his chest. But while tiny in stature, he noted all the female attributes that would easily attract the attention of any red-blooded male. High, firm breasts were enhanced by a narrow waist and a beautifully shaped caboose.

"You needn't worry, ma'am. He'll not bother you again. I'll personally see to it."

She released her grip on his arms, leaned away, reached into a pocket somewhere in the folds of her gray dress, then dabbed at red-rimmed eyes with a tiny square of white cloth. "I barely knew the brute. We met on the stage from Jacksboro this very morning."

"I'm sure you're aware that such casual meetings can sometimes prove most unfortunate in this day and time. Evil men roam the countryside like hungry animals."

"But he was most gracious. And when we arrived in town, he insisted that I accompany him to dinner. I tried to explain that my stage east would leave before we could possibly finish, but he would not listen. He grabbed my arm and virtually dragged me along with him."

"Why didn't you call out? I'm confident there are plenty of men who'd be more than willing to help a beautiful woman—even in a place like Hell's Half Acre."

She sniffled, then said, "He told me, in no uncertain terms, that if I caused any problem, the consequences would be most severe. Given the circumstances, I believed him."

"Well, I must admit that your response was more than understandable."

"As soon as we got seated inside the White Elephant, he started drinking. His personality changed so quickly. I've never before witnessed such an amazing, and frightening, transformation. And worse, I found the ill will that came out of the man impossible to fathom."

Longarm turned the girl and pointed her north toward Second Street. "Let's stroll a few blocks, take in the evening air. You can catch your breath. Sure it'll help settle your nerves."

As they passed the glass-paned, carpeted entry to the Centennial Theater, she said, "I heard that dapper, well-dressed little gentleman in the White Elephant call you Marshal Long."

"Yes." He bowed slightly, tipped his hat, then said, "Forgive my ill-mannered negligence, ma'am. The heat of the moment appears to have left me a bit inattentive, I think. Deputy U.S. Marshal Custis Long, your obedient servant."

She stroked his arm. "Please don't call me ma'am, or missus. Those terms make me feel so old. My name is Matilda Wayland. My friends know me as Mattie. I'd be pleased if you called me Mattie, as well, Marshal Long."

"Mattie?"

"Yes."

"I like it."

At the corner of Fort Worth's Main and Second, she leaned against him as though they were lovers, then let her head rest on his upper arm. "Wish I'd never spoken to the man. My mother taught me better. My God, what must I have been thinking?" she mumbled.

"Say you met him on the Jacksboro stage?"

"Yes, I'd made the connection from Wichita Falls on my way to visit family in Tyler."

As they stepped onto the boardwalk in front of the El Paso Hotel, Longarm said, "Quite a long trip for an unescorted lady, don't you think? Wouldn't it have been better to travel in the company of an attendant or relative?"

"No," she said. "I've never considered my solitary travels as any immediate threat to my person. I've made this exact same journey a number of times before, and met many other men on the coach without incident."

"You just never know about people, Mattie."

"I suppose. Truly, nothing seemed amiss on this outing, until that horrible beast forced me to accompany him to dinner. Of course, I protested his surly treatment, but my complaints fell on deaf ears. Worse, his brutish actions have caused me to miss my stage. My bags must be halfway to Tyler by now. All I have with me is my purse. And there won't be another coach for two days. I have no inkling what I'll do for a place to spend the night in peace and safety."

As their comfortable stroll continued, Longarm said, "No doubt about it, you've had a difficult evenin', Mattie."

"I do believe that the worst part of the whole experience came after we sat down at the table in the restaurant. That's when his insistent and bold behavior got completely out of hand. The more he drank, the more profane and suggestive he became."

"Did you even know the man's name?"

"He called himself Quincy Ballentine."

Longarm stopped dead in his tracks, pulled the woman to a halt at his side, then gazed back down the street toward the entry of the White Elephant. "You're sure about that, Mattie? Quincy Ballentine? Sweet Jesus."

"Do you know the horrible swine, Mr. Long?"

"Indeed, Mattie. I know the horrible swine. Didn't recognize him."

Chapter 8

Longarm turned and gazed down at the woman. "Well, let's just say that I know *of* the horrible swine. And what I know isn't good, by any measure available to reasonable people. He's a bad'un. His cadre of friends might well be even worse—if such a thing is possible. Makes me think Luke Short could've been right. Maybe I shoulda just gone ahead and killed the rotten skunk while I had the upper hand."

"Oh, my word. You mean he's that depraved an individual?"

"He is indeed. Quincy Ballentine's rotten to the core and perhaps a lot worse."

She fanned her face with the tiny handkerchief. "But he seemed so pleasant while we were on the stage. Most gracious, and friendly to a fault. Well behaved, even. No problems whatsoever."

"What did you say, back there in the restaurant? Do you remember what set 'im off?"

Several seconds of silence passed before she whispered, "Let's just leave it with the fact that he made a number of indecent proposals."

Longarm stopped on the boardwalk and turned her to face him again. "Look, Mattie, I just pistol-whipped the bejabbers out of a man I don't really even know for behavior I found repulsive that he directed toward a beautiful woman. Cannot abide any man who'd slap a woman in public, or anywhere else for that matter. But I need to know exactly what he said to you, and why he felt compelled to strike you with such enthusiasm—twice."

She dropped her gaze and refused to look him in the eye. "I'm such a goose. I should have known what to expect of a drunkard. Actually, now that I think about it, he started pouring the liquor down as soon as we stepped off the stage. And even though he'd bullied me into having dinner with him and caused me to miss my connection, I didn't get terribly concerned about his growing belligerence until we were almost done with our meal. That's when he exploded and turned brutally hostile."

A degree of impatience tinged Longarm's voice when he snapped, "But what did he say to you, Mattie?"

"He suggested that we retire to the nearest hotel room and . . . and . . . well, he wanted me to, you know, service him."

"Jesus."

A certain amount of strange excitement seemed to tinge her voice when she breathlessly added, "And he wasn't shy about the kind of *sexual* favors he expected from me, either, Custis. He described, in the most graphic detail, while we sat right there at the table, exactly what he required."

"And you said no."

"Well, of course I said no. Twice. He hit me both

times. I mean, gracious, the meal was nice, but is an un-
sophisticated country girl required to do just anything a
strange man can think of for a plate of victuals and a
glass of cheap wine?" She picked at a button on Longarm's vest and swayed back and forth like a teasing little girl. "Then you came over to the table like some kind
of knight in shining armor from a romantic novel and
rescued me."

As their walk turned back south, they passed the
Club Room Saloon and Ten Pin Alley. Longarm pulled
a cheroot from his vest and lit it. He shook the match
out, flicked it into the street, then said, "Might be difficult to get you a room this late in the day. Bet every
hotel in town is filled to the brim by now."

Mattie squeezed his arm. The excitement bubbled up
again when she said, "Why, Marshal Long, are you sug-
gesting that I spend the night with you? Wherever that
might be?"

"Why, I wouldn't dare make any such suggestion."

"Why not?"

The boldness of her question surprised Longarm, but
he tried not to show the growing interest that had begun
to burn somewhere just below the buckle of his pistol
belt.

"See here, Mattie, I have a large room at the El Paso
Hotel, across the street from the White Elephant. I'll be
in Fort Worth for about a week, and will be more than
happy to share those quarters with you until such time
as you can get back on the road to your family."

She squeezed his arm once more. "That's so very
kind of you, Custis. And since I'm a woman alone, with
nowhere else to turn, I'm inclined to accept your offer."

"Good enough. Come along, then, and we'll get the sleeping arrangements settled and make all the necessary preparations to see to your comfort while you're in town."

Longarm walked Matilda Wayland across Third Street, through the El Paso's elegant lobby, and directly past the busy reception counter. He tipped his hat at the hotel's clearly fascinated desk clerk, who nodded back and smiled knowingly but made no move to object to a paying guest's selection for company.

Longarm ushered Mattie into his room, threw his hat on the chest of drawers, then went to each of the windows and pulled the curtains closed. He lit a fancy oil lamp covered by an etched glass shade, but left the wick low. As he shook the match to nothing more than a smoking cinder, he felt the stunning girl come up behind him. Her arms encircled his waist, and firm, melon-sized breasts pressed against his back. An inquisitive hand slid down the front of his pants, then squeezed.

She hugged him close, then pulled him around to face her. A moist tongue flicked over crimson, parted lips. She brought her hips up in a provocative move that pressed her sex against the rapidly responding member behind the crotch of his pants. "I've been thinking," she hissed.

He smiled, bent over, playfully nibbled her neck, licked her ear, then said, "Have you, now? And what exactly have you been thinking, darlin'?"

Mattie inserted an inquisitive finger inside the front of his shirt, then tickled a spot on his bare chest while he went back to nibbling at all the tender, sensitive spots he could find. "I've been thinking that I owe you a debt of gratitude I will probably never be able to fully repay, Custis." She hesitated, pushed him back, gazed into his eyes, then added, "No matter what I do."

He shook his head. "Now, look, Mattie. You don't owe me anything. And besides, I've never been one to take liberties with a lady who finds herself in such a state of terrible disadvantage the way you have."

"You can't take liberties if I'm willing." She moaned, then pulled his face down to hers with both hands and pressed a wet, inviting mouth to his. Her tongue slid over his lips as she broke the open-mouthed kiss. "Can you?"

Longarm slid a hand down one of the flushed girl's muscular buttocks, the other up to a waiting breast, and squeezed both at the same time. He pulled her to the perfect spot, then hunched forward and rubbed his cock against her grinding crotch.

"I suppose not," he breathed into her ear. "But let's be clear on this matter. You're absolutely sure you want to go through with what you've just implied?"

She gasped, made a moaning, mewling sound, then pushed his arms aside, stepped away, and in a single, practiced move shucked her dress. Soon, the crisp, ruffled blouse and all her undergarments, except for a pair of fancy embroidered silk open-crotched pantalets, lay in a rumpled pile on the floor. Totally bare from the waist up, she looked smaller, and younger. Giggling like a child, she took two bounding steps and jumped onto the bed.

Longarm watched, wide-eyed, as Mattie rolled onto her back, raised perfect legs into the air, caressed herself, top and bottom, then beckoned for him to hurry. The thought flashed across his mind that Mattie Wayland seemed just a bit too professional for the innocent she had first appeared to be. But he quickly dismissed the thought and began removing his own clothing. As he ripped at his vest and shirt, she tore a pair of skin-tight underpants away, laughed, and threw them at him. He could smell the ripe muskiness of her on the hand-sized garment when he pulled it off his shoulder and dropped it atop her other clothing.

Longarm's brown tweed coat, vest, and blue-gray shirt quickly formed a second heap at the foot of the bed. He kicked low-heeled boots across the room, then pushed his high-waisted, near-skin-tight pants down.

Mattie squirmed on the sheets like she was lying on a bed of red-hot coals. She caressed her breasts, pushed one up, craned her neck forward, and nibbled at the nipple. She switched to the other nipple and watched, wide-eyed and fascinated, when his massive, rigid cock escaped the confines of his tweed pants, flipped up, and slapped against his flat belly with a resounding *plop*.

Her words sounded like shots from a Gatling gun. She yelped, "Come on, come on, come on," then she raised her legs and used two fingers to open herself for him. "Fuck me like it's the last time you'll ever do it, Custis, and for the love of God, hurry."

An animalistic grin creaked across his face. Longarm climbed onto the bed, then knelt between the hunching girl's shapely legs. A flush of pink excitement covered her besotted face and shoulders. He leaned forward slightly and rubbed the stiff shaft and fist-sized head of his cock against her waiting, pink wetness. He kept the tease going while she moaned, clawed at his gyrating hips, and grabbed for the rampant beast between them.

When the agitated girl began to whimper like a whipped dog, pinch at her own nipples, and finger herself with increasing urgency, he plunged forward and down—into volcanic, velvety depths that gushed and squirted around the shaft of his taut dong. The sound her succulent pussy made spurred him to an eruption of frantic, grinding thrusts that went as deep as he could drive himself into her receptive body. The massaging vibration that erupted from her steaming sex kept him going, as surely as if she'd been wearing Mexican rowels the size of gold double eagles, and raked his flanks like a south Texas cowgirl breaking a wild stallion.

Mattie arched her back to meet Longarm's every thrust into the center of her being. She clawed her way down his back, latched onto steely buttocks like a sharp-clawed cat in heat, and tried to match his energetic pounding with an equal and vigorous upward lunge of her own. She let go of his pile-driving ass long enough to pull at her own nipples again, then closed her eyes in orgasmic ecstasy. After a minute or so, her eyes popped open. She pushed her boobs—reddened by her own pawing and pinching—up as high as she could and watched as he licked and sucked at nipples that took on the size of a man's thumb from all the rough encouragement they'd endured.

Longarm drew his mouth away from the astonishing tips of Mattie's tits with a lurid, sucking smack. She let out a wicked cackling laugh, bucked like a wild animal, threw her arms around his neck, and in a move that belied the petite girl's size and strength, wrestled him onto his back. When she slid down his enormous love muscle, then bounced up and down on it like a crazed marionette controlled by some unseen, insane puppeteer hiding above them, her flashing eyes appeared to roll into the top of her skull. A rosy flush tinted her glistening shoulders and neck. Rivers of sweat cascaded down between jiggling breasts. Several times she leaned forward and smeared her steaming, wet nipples over his mouth and moaned when he sucked them.

After several minutes of a feverish assault, the sex-crazed girl hopped off his saber-hard tool, swung her legs around, sat on his face, and wiggled her well-formed ass. No doubt existed as to what she wanted and clearly expected. With a tongue like a magic wand, Longarm soon had her producing sounds like a box full of cute little baby piglets. But the squealing lasted only a short time. She latched onto his cock, ran a tongue of flame around his balls, then licked her way up and down the shaft. She got as much of it as possible into her mouth, then sucked like a thing possessed.

Eventually the overpowering urge to bring their carnal wrestling match to its logical climax overtook Longarm in a rush of urgent need. He pushed Mattie away, turned her back around, climbed between her flailing legs, plunged into her juicy sweetness again, and immediately emptied his entire being inside the girl's scorching hot interior.

Exhausted from a long day's events, Longarm rolled to one side and closed his eyes. Mattie Wayland's still-glowing body was nestled in the crook of a tired arm. His last conscious memory of the night's lusty tussle came when the stunning girl turned on her side and pushed her still overheated ass against his semirigid cock. He slipped inside her, then drifted into a deep, satisfying nap.

At some point during the night, the usually vigilant

Longarm would later remember that he came partially awake and thought he heard Mattie Wayland stirring around the dark room. Anticipating nothing unusual in such typically female activity, he groaned, rolled onto his stomach, placed a feather pillow over his head to blot out the noise, and immediately went back to sleep.

Chapter 9

In spite of the fact that he'd closed the curtains the night before, the next morning's blazing Texas sun sliced through the thin panels of material covering the El Paso Hotel's windows. A knife edge of heavenly flame sliced across the carpet, crept up the side of the bed, then slapped Longarm across the face so hard his eyes popped open like the bullet-blasted hasp on a Wells Fargo strong-box.

He grunted, rolled onto his back, then flung an arm over his face in an effort to block out the brain-piercing light. All of a sudden, he realized how quiet the room seemed. He felt around the bed with his free hand, then sat bolt upright. Blazing daylight slapped him again and forced him to squint his way around the haze-filled room. It appeared that Mattie Wayland had vanished, like a wisp of musky smoke.

He leaned over the edge of the bed and searched the floor for her clothing—gone. Shoes—gone. Not a stitch of anything feminine to be seen anywhere. Then the realization of what had happened hit him like an anvil dropped from heaven's front doorstep. He swung his legs off the bed, hopped up, and padded across the room.

A quick trip to the dressing table revealed that she'd emptied his wallet. The cash he'd carried there—gone. Still naked, he stood in the middle of the room, scratched his head, then his crotch. He threw his head back, chuckled, and to no one in particular mumbled, "Shit. God Almighty, Custis. That hot-assed little gal done gone and rolled your silly behind. Now ain't that a fuckin' wonderment."

By the time he'd got himself fully awake, refreshed, dressed, and ready for the coming day, Longarm had raked over every second of his time with Mattie Wayland the previous night. He stepped onto the El Paso Hotel's shaded, rocking chair–covered veranda, jerked a nickel cheroot from his vest pocket, and lit it.

Within seconds, a grinning Willard Allred hobbled up. He touched the brim of his hat and nodded. "Mornin', Marshal Long. Hope you had a good evenin' and a damn fine night."

Longarm blew a smoke ring toward heaven, arched an eyebrow in Allred's direction, then said, "Well, my evenin' started out pretty good, Willard. Hell, actually started out great, what with our very cordial drink and all. Unfortunately my first night of rest and recuperation in the Gateway to the West eventually resulted in a set of rather surprising and unpleasant circumstances."

A puzzled look flitted across Allred's bedraggled face. He scratched a stubble-covered chin that hadn't seen a straight razor in weeks, then said, "Uh, last night didn't work out too well after we parted, I take it."

Longarm gazed at the street as though he didn't see any of the people, horses, wagons, dogs, or constant movement that raised a thick, hazy curtain of dust between the hotel and the White Elephant Saloon. He puffed at the cheroot. "Well, that's actually a bit of a fuckin' understatement, Willard. Damned good-lookin' little gal I took up with in the Elephant's restaurant went and bilked me outta all the cash I had in my wallet. Fortunately, she was either in too big a hurry or wasn't smart enough to get into the wardrobe and go through my possibles bag. Never carry much real money on my person, 'less it can't be avoided. As a consequence, thank God, she didn't get much."

A fleeting grin flickered across Allred's face, then quickly disappeared. He pulled at one corner of his moustache, then said, "You gonna sic Marshal Farmer and his bunch of bruisers on 'er? Personally wouldn't advise it, but you go on an' do what you have to do."

Longarm shook his head, then toed at a nail sticking out of the plank at his feet. "No. Doubt I'll bring Farmer into this mess, Tater. Figure to take care of the whole shootin' match myself. Be willin' to bet she and that skunk I whacked in the Elephant were in cahoots. Guess my actions, when we met, musta been somethin' of a surprise to both of 'em. But by God that didn't stop her from damn near fuckin' my eyeteeth out, then takin' all my walkin'-around money and vanishin' like spit on a Montana railroad depot's stove lid."

"You the one what took a pistol barrel to Quincy Ballentine's double-thick thinker box last night?"

"Yep. The very one."

"Ah. And the little gal what fucked you, then robbed you, she was with him at the time?"

"There you go."

The words had barely escaped Tater Allred's lips

when one of Marshal Farmer's Fort Worth policemen—
a man Longarm recognized from his visit to the jail the
day before—strolled up and tipped his black slouch hat.
"Mornin' gents." He immediately focused on Longarm,
then said, "The marshal sent me to fetch you over to ole
Doc Wheeler's office."

"Fetch me over?"

"Yep. Said for me to tell you that he needs to talk
with you. Kinda urgent-like."

Longarm flicked an inch of gray ash from his
panatela, then turned to Allred. "You know where this
Doc Wheeler's office is, Tater?"

"Sure. Everybody in town knows Doc. He's got a
storefront operation up on the corner of Rusk Street and
Weatherford—door or two down from the Texas Express Company. Real easy ride from here. Couldn't be
more'n three or four blocks altogether."

Longarm swung his attention back to Farmer's
deputy. "Your boss say what he wants?"

The deputy dipped his head and looked sneaky.
"Well, Marshal, sir, to be truthful, I do know why he
had me come for you. But he said I was not to tell. Only
to say it were urgent and he's sure you'll be interested in
what he's got to show you."

Longarm thumped the unfinished stub of his cheroot
into the street. "Where's your wagon, Tater?"

"Over yonder 'cross the street, Marshal Long. See it.
She's parked in front of the Empress Saloon."

Longarm plowed through the flow of traffic along
Main Street. Allred and Farmer's deputy followed like
small boats in the wake of a larger, more threatening
ship. Longarm hopped onto the seat of the wagon, then

made a motion like a cavalry officer ordering a charge as Allred climbed up beside him. "Hop on, Deputy," Longarm said. "Can't wait to see what this early morning summons is all about."

The short trip up Main, then east on an even busier and dustier Weatherford Street, took less than five minutes. At the corner of Rusk, Longarm jumped off the wagon before it came to a complete stop. A painted sign with gold lettering over the door welcomed visitors to the office of Doctor John Wheeler. Longarm burst through the doorway like a man on a mission.

Marshal Sam Farmer and a wizened, pinch-faced gent wearing a worn look, wire-rimmed goggles, and a frayed three-piece suit, white shirt, and string tie sat at a scar-covered desk just inside the door. Both men nursed cups of strong-smelling coffee, while hand-rolled cigarettes between their fingers wafted threads of smoke toward the ceiling.

Overloaded and overflowing glass-front lawyer's bookcases stood against almost every inch of viewable wall space. Many of the shelves contained assortments of patent medicines in a wide variety of brightly colored glass bottles that sported even more colorful and picturesque labels.

Tables, shoved into the corners, contained carefully laid-out displays of polished steel medical instruments that resembled the horrifying tools of medieval torture. The cramped room reeked with the combined odors of carbolic, alcohol, and an additional nose-twitching stench Longarm couldn't quite place—something between human feces and the fetid reek of puke.

Directly behind the weathered desk, two closed

doors led into what Longarm surmised had to be examination rooms, which could be closed off to render a bit of privacy, if needed.

Farmer stood and made the necessary introductions. As Tater Allred and the Fort Worth deputy crowded inside, Farmer said, "Doc's got a badly injured patient in the room yonder who asked to see you, Marshal."

"Me? Asked to see me? You're sure?"

"Yep. Lady said I was to send for Marshal Custis Long, stayin' at the El Paso Hotel. Even knew your room number. She's laid out in the stall on the left."

" 'She'? You said 'she,' right?"

"Yep. One of my deputies found her, 'bout daylight. Somebody'd dumped her like a pile of trash in the alley between the Theatre Comique and the Centennial Theater."

"Found her? What exactly does that mean, Sam?"

Farmer looked uncomfortable, then waved at the door again. " 'Pears as how the same somebody who dumped her stomped the unmerciful hell outta the poor girl. My deputy musta come on the tragic scene right after the sorry deed happened. Why don't you go on in? I'm sure the lady can clear up all your questions. She's been beat up pretty bad, but she can still talk. Even appears anxious to do so."

Longarm snatched his hat off, worked his way around Farmer, past the silent, dyspeptic-looking doctor and the desk, then pushed the flimsy door open. He stepped inside a small, stuffy, nigh airless room, then closed the wobbly entry panel behind him as quietly as he could.

A low, couchlike affair, draped in brilliantly white sheets, stood against the wall on the far side of the room. It almost appeared to glow in the dim light provided by a single window covered with a black oilcloth shade. Two more steps brought him right up beside the improvised bed, which rested near the foot of a shabby, well-used examining table.

Longarm leaned over and strained for several seconds before he recognized the sleeping woman on the bed. Mattie Wayland's face was a badly abused mess, covered in blue-black bruises and dried blood tinged with a thin layer of an orange-tinted antiseptic—probably iodine, he thought. A split, stitched brow heightened a blackened right eye almost swollen shut. Numerous other ugly contusions decorated her forehead, neck, and ears. The angry, reddish imprints of a man's knuckles glowed from beneath the unsightly patchwork of injuries. Shocked by her appearance, he reached down and touched her hand.

A crashing wave of fury swept through Longarm's entire being. Embarrassed and enraged by the sorry evidence of such inhuman treatment, he glanced away from Mattie's maltreated face. For several seconds he stared at a framed diploma on the wall, which attested to Doctor John Wheeler's graduation from a well-known medical college in New Orleans. He rubbed throbbing temples, then let his gaze come back down to the mass of bruises and cuts that had smiled and called his name in ecstasy only a few hours before.

After he jiggled her blood-flecked fingers a time or two, the battered girl stirred. She worked hard to hold open eyes shot through with spiderwebs of red, then gazed up at her visitor. At first he could barely hear the whispery rasp that clawed its way past split, swollen lips. The words came out slow, hesitant, and gritty with pain. "Custis. I'm so pleased . . . you came. Realize I had no right to expect such kindness . . . but I'm glad you're here."

Longarm kneeled beside the bed. He held Mattie's hand in his, then shook his head in disbelief. In a voice tinged with regret, concern, and carefully controlled anger, he growled, "What happened, darlin'? Who did this to you? Do you know? Can you tell me?"

Labored breathing preceded her tortured reply. "Quincy. Who else? Blamed me . . . for the . . . pistol-whippin' you gave . . . him at the Elephant. Caught me. Outside the hotel. Thought I . . . was dead—wished for death. Never been hurt like this . . . before, Custis. Never."

Longarm used a single finger to push aside a wisp of blood-encrusted hair that dangled from beneath a stained bandage wrapped around her head. "The two of you were workin' together at some kinda bunko cheat on me at the White Elephant, weren't you?"

Mattie's voice seemed to strengthen a bit when she said, "Yes. Figured to . . . turn your head . . . steal whatever I could. Hoped to drug you . . . at the first . . . opportunity. Laudanum in your liquor. Plan didn't work out the way . . . Quincy expected."

In her brutalized condition, Longarm knew the girl would likely have trouble understanding. As slowly as possible, he said, "Quincy was supposed to act shocked and surprised that anyone would come to your aid, then somehow beat a hasty retreat. Leave you to the concerned care of the poor sucker who came to save you from a heartless brute. Was that the way of it? The plan?"

"Yes. But he felt I . . . overplayed my part . . . said I'd flirted too much. Played innocent too well. Caused the wrong man's . . . surprising response. You broke . . . a couple of his teeth off."

Longarm chuckled. "Guess the way I bounced my pistol off his cheek probably did come as something of a shock to the stupid cocksucker."

"Shocked me," Mattie whispered. Then she appeared to regain some strength. "We've run . . . the same dodge, at one time or another, in Texas, Kansas . . . all over. Usually when Quincy's short of money. No one ever . . . knocked Quincy out . . . of his chair before. You just didn't give him . . . time to turn tail. Retreat. 'Course . . . might have . . . overplayed his . . . own part a bit, too."

"A bit? Hell, girl, he slapped the hell out of you. Twice. Right in public. Must admit, I'm shocked and dismayed by the fact that I could be so easily fooled. Should have known better. But, by God, what he did got under my skin and got him exactly what he deserved."

Mattie groaned, then snorted. "Vanity makes all you men so unbelievably stupid. You're so easy. So . . . predictable. Led by your cocks like randy stallions. Takin' . . . advantage of dumb-assed men, who get a hard-on . . . every time a breeze blows across their crotches, is the . . . easiest work an ambitious female can get."

"Well, now that might well be a bit strong. Sometimes the particular woman who brings the breeze does make a difference."

A bloodshot gaze scanned his face. A tiny smile crimped the corner of her mouth. "All a woman's . . . gotta do . . . is breathe in the general direction of a man's cock, and he'll follow her anywhere. Crawl around on his hands and knees . . . howl like a dog . . . if she asks him to do it."

Longarm stared at his own feet and nodded. "Well, suppose some of that's true enough. When it comes to good-lookin' women blessed with an easy attitude toward sex, most of us don't exercise much in the way of good judgment."

A timid smile creased Mattie's swollen lips. "You're a novelty, Marshal."

"How so?"

"Believe you're the first . . . I've ever known willing to own up . . . to his shortcomings."

With as much tenderness as he could muster, Longarm stroked Mattie's bandaged head. "Best not to use the word *short* with most men, darlin'. Does have a way of deflatin' any feller who's inclined to be deflated. Now tell me, how many times have you done this before?"

Mention of her past misdeeds appeared to rouse her even more. "Hundreds, Custis. Me'n Quincy've made a mountain of money off lesser men than you. Men who wound up with a sore head and an empty wallet." She squeezed the fingers of his hand. Her eyes watered. "Sometimes . . . I fucked 'em so they'd be happy . . . Rare, but it happened. Usually . . . did just enough to keep 'em busy till the drugs went to work."

"What about you and me?"

The tiny smile reappeared. "That was a first. Must admit . . . I became excited far beyond words, once we were alone. Something about you, darlin'. Something I can't explain. You remind me of someone I knew, I think. Loved, or was attracted to and didn't know why at the time. Haven't felt . . . that way . . . in years. Guess it all caught up with me . . . last night."

She appeared to collapse. Longarm knew he needed

to bring the conversation to a quick end. "You know where Quincy is now, Mattie?"

Her eyes closed, and for several seconds Longarm thought perhaps she'd passed out or drifted off to sleep. But then she squeezed his hand again and said, "Can't . . . say for absolute sure. Doubt he's left town. Quincy likes all the doin's down in the Acre. Loves to . . . gamble . . . drink, and whore around. Says he gets tired of fuckin' me. Needs some *strange* every once in a while."

"Does the son of a bitch have a favorite spot he likes to frequent over all the others?"

Mattie squirmed as though uncomfortable. A pained grimace etched deep lines beneath the flaked blood still pasted on her battered face. "Prefers Mary Porter's. Best-lookin' girls in Texas. Near Josie Belmont's. Jesse Reeves's joint, too. Likes to have drinks at the Two Minnies Saloon. Place with the glass ceilin' . . . where you can look up at the nekkid girls on the floor above. Puts up at the Drover's Inn sometimes, too." She turned away and appeared to drop off to sleep again.

Longarm placed a reassuring hand on the girl's shoulder. "Rest now, Mattie darlin'. I'll find the worthless son of a bitch, and when I do, he'll wish his mother'd never squeezed him out."

Longarm stormed back through Doc Wheeler's office. Didn't stop until he was able to stand on the boardwalk and breathe something other than the dense, choking, miasmic cloud that saturated the local pill wrangler's entire space. As he fired up an aromatic cheroot soaked in Kentucky bourbon, the other men filed out the door and gathered around him in a concerned knot.

Through a blur of fresh, sweet-smelling tobacco

smoke, Longarm said, "Way you had her patched up and covered, I'm sure all I could see was just the most superficial part of her injuries. So tell me, Doc, how bad's she really hurt? What's the total of the damage?"

Wheeler squinted, toed at the board under his foot. He pulled his spectacles off and tapped them against the palm of his hand. "Well, Marshal, her left arm is broken, just above the elbow. Looks like the guy who thrashed her did it with his fists. She has at least a couple of broken ribs on the same side. Appears to me her attacker might have knocked the lady down, then kicked hell out of her. Series of unsightly contusions all over her back and legs brought me to that particular diagnosis. And, perhaps worst, she could well be suffering from a serious concussion. Hard to tell right now."

Longarm took his hat off and slapped it against his leg. Tater Allred gazed into the street like a man hypnotized by the passing of a fancy carriage and team. Marshal Sam Farmer glanced at his deputy, then made a flicking motion with one hand that freed the man to hustle away from the scene and head off to the west, back along Weatherford.

"Reckon she's gonna live, Doc?" Longarm glared at the medicine man, as though daring him to answer the question the wrong way.

"Wish I had a crystal ball, but that's impossible to know, Marshal Long. I wouldn't even venture a guess at this juncture. Man who beat this lady did the most concentrated, thorough job I've ever seen in all my years of practice. He meant for the thumping she got to hurt, and for a long time to come. Whatever her future state of health might hold, I can say she's gonna be very uncomfortable for months to come down the road."

A steely-eyed gaze turned on Sam Farmer. "Want you to do me a favor, Marshal," Longarm grunted.

Farmer forced a tight smile. "If I can."

"Oh, you can. But that's not the problem. Problem is, will you?"

"Well, spit it out, Custis. Whatta you want? Give me a hint."

All ears and eyes turned Longarm's direction. "Want you to let me handle this mess, Sam. Keep your boys out of it. Sure they've got more'n enough to do anyhow. Tell 'em to give Quincy Ballentine, and any of his henchmen who might be in town, or show up, plenty of room. Want to play out an ample amount of rope for 'em. Then, I'm gonna personally hang 'em."

Farmer stared into the twin muzzles of a pair of blue-gray eyes for about ten seconds, then blinked. "Alright. I'll give you your head on this. At least for a spell, anyway. But only because you're right in your assessment of our workload."

A slight smile turned the corners of Longarm's mouth up. "One other favor."

Marshal Farmer shoved his thumbs into the waist of his pants and reared back on his heels. "Yeah. And just what in the hell would that be?"

"Move her to my room in the El Paso. She'll be safer. I can keep a closer eye on her. Doubt Quincy's smart enough to figure out where we might hide her. Send a nurse along to watch over things in my absence. I'll pay the freight. Then get your people together and tell 'em what we've agreed to do."

"I can do that. All of it."

"Wait a minute, Marshal Long," Doc Wheeler said. "I can't allow you to move my patient. Not right now, anyway. Maybe in two or three days or so, perhaps longer. But right now, such an action is out of the question. She's in a terrible and delicate condition. An inexperienced nurse, because that's all you'll get around here, is out of the question until such time as I can determine just how bad off she really is."

Longarm ran a hand over the back of his neck as though he had a pain he couldn't quite locate. "Understood, Doc. I'll figure out something else. Might have to put a guard on her for a few days. Because you can bet your stethoscope, Quincy'll try to kill her once he finds out I'm after him and that he didn't manage to do it last night."

"Anything else?" Farmer said.

Longarm jerked a thumb toward Tater. "Let your men know that Willard Allred will be helping me, and that they should look on him as my personally appointed special deputy in this matter."

Farmer threw a quick glance in Tater Allred's direction, nodded, then said, "If that's what you want. Sure, I'll take care of it."

Longarm clapped Fort Worth's chief lawman on the shoulder, then shook his hand. "This dance might get real nasty 'fore it's over and done, Sam. But trust me, whatever happens, there'll be a good reason for all of it."

A puzzled look flashed across Farmer's face. He slowed the handshake. With some hesitation in his voice, he said, "I totally understand your feelings on this matter, Marshal Long. Got no use for a man who'd do such things to a woman, myself. Unfortunately, similar events take place in the Acre almost weekly. Difficult to impossible to stop 'em. So you do as you see fit,

Marshal Long. We'll sort out any repercussions when this dance is all done. How's that sound to you?"

Longarm nodded, then turned and headed for Tater Allred's wagon. Over his shoulder he said, "Just capital, by God, Marshal Farmer. Capital." Once in the wagon's seat, he called out to Doc Wheeler, "We'll leave Mattie here until you deem it safe to move her, Doc. Make damned sure you take good care of the lady. See to it she gets whatever she requires. I'll stand good for any cost." He turned to Willard and said, "Let's go to the Elephant. Stand you to another drink. Know for damned sure I could use a glass of Maryland rye right now. Maybe even a double."

Chapter 10

Longarm leaned on the White Elephant's polished mahogany bar. An overwhelming weariness pervaded his being. He poured a shot of amber-colored bourbon, then shoved it toward Willard Allred. Allred snatched up the glass, downed the liquor in one quick gulp, and, grinning, pushed the tiny beaker back with a single finger.

"Special deputy. Ain't that somethin'. Been a spell since anyone bothered to express the slightest kind of faith in me, Marshal Long," Allred said. "Want you to know I'll do my best in whatever endeavor you choose to have me take on." He picked up his refilled glass, saluted, then downed the second shot as quickly as the first. "First time I've felt like a man in a spell and, I gotta tell you, it feels damned good."

On the third round, both men gave their waiting glasses of nose paint a brief rest. They leaned against the bar and gazed into the White Elephant's enormous silvered mirror. Longarm watched the beautiful hostess reflected in the mirror as she guided guests into the dining room for a late breakfast or an early lunch.

"Tater, I'd never seen Quincy Ballentine before I whacked him the other night. Heard enough of him, but we'd never met face-to-face. Funny thing is, all the stories about the man, as I'm familiar with, didn't involve anything like the sorry bastard being a pimp and confidence artist. Kinda scum who'd use a good-lookin' woman to steal from unsuspecting men with big eyes and a hard-on."

Allred grinned. "Well, as my ole pappy used to say, skunks is skunks. And them as is skunks will do anything to get their hands on a little money. Wouldn't put it past ole Quincy to rob the offerin' plate at a church, given the chance.

"Well, that don't make him much different than a good many around these days."

"Given the way the truth suffers at the hands of writers these days, just about anybody can get a reputation as a badman. But the real truth bein' what it is, though, ole Quincy ain't never been much more'n a pimp, as far as I've ever known. 'Course he does seem to be able to keep company with some real bad actors, though. Hard to know why or how, but he seems to be able to get dangerous men to do his biddin'. Must have something of the leader in 'im as most of us can't see."

Longarm leaned closer to his new deputy. "Think you can find the son of a bitch? He doesn't know we're connected, at least not yet, anyway. As a consequence, I think you can move around down in the Acre and find out a good deal more, and a lot quicker, than I probably could."

Allred nodded, scratched his stubble-covered chin, looked thoughtful for a second, then said, "The Acre ain't real big, you know. But they's lots of places to hide. Town's like a rat's warren. Might take a day or two, but I'll find him, if'n he's still around."

"Oh, I doubt he's bothered to leave. I'm of the firm opinion that he figures to have killed Mattie. Doesn't know yet that she's still alive, and I want to keep it that way till we can find him."

Allred stared into the full glass of liquor on the bar. He twirled the drink around in a tiny circle of liquid puddled beneath it. "Man travels in some pretty rough company, Marshal Long."

"Call me Custis, or better yet, my friends call me Longarm."

"Longarm?"

"Yep. If you're the type who's one of those folks that society needs to jack up the jail and put you under it, the long arm of the law's gonna snatch your ass up and make you pay. I'm that long arm of the law."

"Ah, well, Longarm, not for dead certain sure, but they's men in the Acre that a lotta folks claim are close associates of ole Quincy's. So far, the whole bunch has kept pretty low to the ground. If'n anyone knows where he is, it'll be one of them ole boys as he keeps company with."

Longarm held up his glass, then clicked it against Allred's. Another shot went down, and the fourth one got poured.

"Who and how many, Tater?"

"Well, one of them as I know of is that one-eyed humpback, Silas Brakett. Ole Silas is bad enough, but then there's that back-shootin' weasel from Georgia, Dead Eyed Zeke Cobb. But by far the worst of 'em might be Tanner Hackberry."

Longarm's eyes snapped shut. His chin dropped down

till it touched his chest. He shook his head, glanced back at Allred, then said, "Jesus, you're sure about that? You're sure Tanner Hackberry's in town?"

"Seen 'im. Seen 'im my very own self. Had a fare from the depot what wanted to go to the Red Light Saloon and Dance Hall down on Rusk. Rough joint not far from the Emerald—place we passed on the way in yesterday."

"Yeah, remember that'n. Didn't look much like an emerald to me."

"Anyhow, stopped outside and walked my fare into the saloon. Introduced him to the drink slinger there, friend of mine—Buster Coody. Buster fixed the feller up with a buck-toothed whore of my acquaintance, widely sought out for her ability to suck the silver plate off a pistol barrel."

Longarm chuckled. "Sweet Jesus. Wouldn't mind meetin' her myself."

"Yeah, well, I wuz a-standin' at the bar when I spotted this big ole boy who'd staked out one whole end of the counter down next to the entrance of the dance hall. Mean-lookin' son of a bitch. Kinda cold-eyed scum that just oozes trouble. Whispered at Buster and asked who he wuz. Buster says, 'Tanner Hackberry. Best stay away from him.' Seemed like mighty good advice at the time."

"God Almighty, that's the truth, Willard. Hackberry's the kind that'll give small children nightmares for the rest of their tender lives. He's a man killer of the first water."

"Heard tell as how he once cut off a man's sack— made himself a purse. Wore it around his neck a-danglin' from a piece of braided horsehide. Gives me the willies just thinkin' 'bout it."

"You think Ballentine might be hangin' around the Red Light with Hackberry and the others?"

Allred eased his glass back over for a refill. Once the glass was full again, he said, "Ain't certain. But it's a good place for all of 'em to lay low while in town, that's for damned sure. One of the roughest places around these days."

"These days?"

"Yeah, Waco Tap used to be the wildest joint in town. When it burnt slap to the ground, the crowd that raised hell over there moved down to the Red Light and the Gilded Lily. Over the past two years or so, that's made the Red Light a damned tough joint to find yourself in once it gets dark. Likewise for the Lily."

"You have any problem hanging around there and keepin' your eyes open?"

"Nope. Bartenders look out for me, kinda like a pet dog with a bad leg."

Longarm slapped the old soldier on the back. "Well then, get on down there and keep an eye out for Quincy or Hackberry or either of them other bastards. Let me know, double quick, if any of 'em shows up. I'm going upstairs. Think I'll spend the evenin' playing poker. Tomorrow you can find me in the El Paso's lobby at the table closest to their bar's batwing doors."

Allred threw down his final shot of bourbon, nodded, came to military attention, did a smartly executed about-face, then headed out the Elephant's front door.

At ten o'clock the following morning, Longarm staked a claim on an overstuffed chair in the El Paso's lobby near the entrance to the hotel's popular saloon. He flopped into the wonderfully comfortable overstuffed seat and, for a while, attempted to scan a copy of the *Fort Worth Daily Democrat* someone had abandoned on a nearby table.

A raging headache, a holdover from the previous evening's protracted poker game, pushed any plans he harbored for an eye-opening glass of rye to a back burner. Instead, he occasionally sipped at his steaming cup of coffee, which a friendly waiter had brought over from the restaurant. The syrupy liquid had been cooked to the consistency of something akin to roofing tar. Longarm sipped, rubbed his temples, and prayed for an end to the darting pain that tortured the inside of his skull.

Eventually, he gave up on the newspaper, leaned back in the chair, placed his hat over his face, and drifted off into a much-needed nap. Gunshots, from somewhere outside the El Paso's door, jerked him out of his pleasantly soothing snooze.

Longarm reacted exactly as any conscientious lawman should. On his feet in an instant, he slapped on his hat and headed toward the action.

He made it to the front door just in time to be pushed aside by a wave of nattering women who elbowed their way past, then headed for the check-in desk and immediately went to chewing the ear of the surprised clerk.

Longarm stopped in the doorway, then stole a quick glance up and down the street. The normally busy thoroughfare seemed to have cleared of most people, but a woman and small child appeared rooted to a spot in the middle of the street less that fifty feet from where he stood. Movement a block away, near the corner of Third and Rusk, drew his attention to at least two men who darted for any available shelter and continued to fire at one another. For several seconds, the blasting got right intense.

Stray bullets kicked up dust and dirt clods near the panic-stricken woman's feet. Longarm hit the street running, snatched up the child, grabbed the lady by the hand, and dragged them to a sheltered spot next to the White Elephant.

As he handed the child over, the lady said, "Oh, thank you, sir. Thank you." She hugged the tot to her ample breast. Hot tears flowed down cheeks bereft of color or rouge. "Don't know what came over me. Just couldn't seem to make my feet move. Felt paralyzed. This is just not the kind of thing you expect on this end of town. Very few street shootings up here away from the Acre."

Longarm's attention shifted from the woman and her child back to the gunfire. None of Marshal Farmer's policemen appeared anywhere in sight. He slipped his Colt Frontier model pistol from its cross-draw holster, snatched off his hat, then peeked up the street toward the noisy disagreement. Men yelled unintelligible threats and curses back and forth at one another, then opened fire again. A horse squealed in pain, reared from the hitch rail, then ran past Longarm's hiding spot and down the street.

He eased onto the boardwalk and took a step toward the action. Over his shoulder, he said, "Stay here, missus. Don't go movin' around in the street until all this indiscriminate shootin' has come to a complete halt."

The belligerent combatants were so preoccupied with their noisy disagreement that neither of them spotted Longarm as he slipped across Main Street, then along the storefronts and saloons to the middle of Third

Street. He landed behind a stack of empty flour barrels piled in front of Harlan's Grocery and Mercantile.

A cowboy, smoking pistol in each hand, stood in the middle of the thoroughfare. With great deliberation, he first fired one pistol, then the other, at a dodging brush popper trying his best to hide behind a water trough on the corner of Rusk Street. Liquid spewed into the street from a number of bullet holes in the wooden horse trough.

After three or four more thunderous reports from the shooters' pistols, Longarm called out, "That's enough boys. You're scarin' the women and children. Not to speak of hittin' horses what don't belong to you."

The shooter in the street made a wobbling turn toward the new threat. Swaying, he tried to make out who'd interrupted his sport. The drunken leather pounder's Mexican spurs made musical, tinkling sounds that drifted toward Longarm's hidey-hole along with a wisp of gray-white, acrid-smelling gunpowder. Hammered silver rowels the size of ten-dollar gold pieces continued to jingle with the man's every inebriated movement.

"Who the fuck're yew, asshole?" the waddie yelped.

The man behind the water trough came to his knees and yelled, "What the hell's goin' on, Cass? Who is that dumb son of a bitch?"

Over his shoulder, and out the side of his mouth, the cow chaser closest to Longarm said, "Don' know who the witless bastard is, Pike." He glared at Longarm and snorted, "Gotta lotta nerve a-goin' an' interruptin' our friendly little disagreementin', mister. Best take yer stringy self back on down the street, 'fore we decide to lay an ass-whoopin' chastisement on yew the likes of what most folks 'round here ain't never seed nor thought about."

Longarm stepped from behind his flour-barrel fortress, badge in hand. He held his silver deputy marshal's star up so the cowboys could see it and said, "I'm the law, you stupid pile of walkin' horseshit. There's been enough of this haphazard gunfire. Gonna say it again—all this lead you're throwin' around is scarin' the hell outta the women, children, and horses, not to mention it's pissin' me off. Now pitch them pistols aside and put your hands in the air. Both of you."

Pike clambered to his feet, then staggered over to Cass's side. Short, stocky, unshaven, and dressed like a rail-riding bum, he was Cass's exact opposite. The pair, who had just tried to kill each other, turned on Longarm, puffed their chests out, and appeared completely willing to go down shooting.

The man called Cass squinted hard, shot a nervous, twitchy-eyed glance in Pike's direction, then said, "Hell, that ain't no real badge. You ain't no real lawman. Lawmen 'round here wear long coats and slouch hats. All of 'em look the same. Ferret-faced ugly and stupider'n a wagonload of flattened shit. Wear big ole six-pointed gold stars pinned on their coats. Damned good targets."

As he swayed drunkenly at the side of the man who'd just been shooting at him, Pike blubbered, "Yeah, yew long, tall glass of skunk piss. 'At 'ere ain't no real badge. An' you ain't no real lawman. So why doanchew go on back where yew came from and just fuck yerself."

Longarm slipped the badge back into his jacket pocket, then said, "I'm a deputy U.S. marshal, and you two jackasses need to pitch them pistols on the ground 'fore you hurt somebody, or get hurt. Damned near hit some folks down the street in front of the El Paso Hotel, and that's two blocks away. Thank God you only managed to wound a horse—so far. Now throw them guns aside and put your hands in the air."

For several seconds the pair exchanged shocked looks and acted confused by the surprising turn of events surrounding their raucous fun. Then, without warning, the weapon in the right hand of the cowboy called Cass went off with a thunderous blast and sent a blue whistler that gouged a massive chunk of wood out of the barrel Longarm stood beside.

Longarm's responding shot caught Cass dead center and pitched him backward. The heavy .45 slug crushed the cowboy's breastbone, bored through his upper body cavity, and exited in a fist-sized gout of blood, bone, and gory spray. He dropped on his side and flopped around like a landed fish for several seconds before coming to a twitching stop.

Pike, stunned and surprised, gazed down at his dead friend for about a second, yelped like a kicked dog, then snatched a second pistol from a holster at his back. Before Longarm could respond, the screeching wrangler hung a curtain of lead in the air that shattered windows in Harlan's Grocery, plowed furrows in the plank boardwalk around Longarm's feet, and blasted holes in the stack of barrels, but failed to come anywhere close to punching a trench in the dodging object of his screaming hatred.

As the wall of blazing slugs moved closer to his position, and appeared about to finally zero in on him, Longarm dropped to one knee, grasped his pistol in both hands, and took careful, steady aim. But before he could squeeze off a death-dealing head shot, a rifle somewhere to his right delivered a chunk of hot lead to Pike's thick noggin that dropped the man in his tracks like a hundred-pound bag of fertilizer kicked off the back of a hoople head's spring wagon.

Longarm darted a glance back toward the El Paso and the White Elephant. Willard Allred stood stock-still in the middle of the street, a smoking Yellow Boy Winchester snugged against his shoulder.

Longarm stood, then strolled over to the bodies lying in the middle of Third Street. Neither man moved. He holstered his weapon, pulled a cheroot from his vest pocket, struck a match on the butt of his pistol, then puffed the tobacco to life. A soul-satisfying cloud of smoke hit his lungs just as Willard Allred ambled up.

"Looked like the feller I put down wuz about to find the right range, Marshal."

Longarm threw his head back and blew a smoke ring toward a crystal blue, cloudless sky. "Yep. Few more seconds and he'd a found me for sure." He slipped another cheroot out and handed it to Willard.

In a matter of seconds, both men savored their cigars and wordlessly thanked God for deliverance from the vagaries of hollow-eyed Death's bony grip. Then Longarm fished a Special Deputy badge out of his pocket and pinned it on Willard's coat lapel. "Just to make it all legal. Consider yourself sworn."

About a minute after the cloud of gunsmoke that hovered over the bloody scene lifted, Sam Farmer and two of his deputies came running up, pistols drawn. "Sweet Jesus, what the hell happened here?" Farmer barked.

As a crowd of inquisitive whisperers and pointers gathered around the dead men, Longarm calmly explained the unfortunate sequence of events that led to one of Fort Worth's busiest thoroughfares being littered with dead bodies. He finished the detailed account with, "Sure hate it, Sam, but me and my special deputy here found it necessary to defend ourselves against a pair of drunken louts who'd have killed us if we had done otherwise."

Farmer looked stricken. "Christ on a crutch, Long. Waddies travelin' through here fire off their weapons all the time. Ain't usually no need to kill 'em."

Longarm dismissed the complaint with a wave of his cigar. "Stupid sons of bitches didn't give us any choice, Sam. Just amble over to that stack of barrels yonder and count the bulletholes. The drunken idiot that Willard put down musta ripped off nigh ten shots before either of us fired back."

Farmer shook his head and toed at the dusty street. "Well, guess it'd be best to have Doc Wheeler conduct a coroner's inquest just to keep things on the up-and-up."

Longarm placed a reassuring hand on Farmer's shoulder. "I'll sit down tonight and write out a full and detailed report on the whole incident. Kind of document that even the U.S. marshal would accept. Sure Doc Wheeler'll be properly impressed. How's that sound?"

Farmer threw Longarm a squinty-eyed glance, then said, "Well, you go right ahead and do that, Marshal. Sure our coroner would be very interested in reading it. Know I would." With that, Farmer motioned his men over. To a tall, thick-necked policeman with a red face he said, "Best go find Doc and get him over here quick as you can, Buster. Me'n Harry'll stay here with the bodies. Hurry up now—let's get this cleared up quick as we can."

Willard Allred pulled at Longarm's sleeve, then

whispered, "Got some news fer you, Marshal. Let's get on away from here so I can tell you."

Longarm and Allred moved away from the carnage. Farmer made no effort to stop their departure. They stopped on the corner of Third just outside the White Elephant's entrance. "Well, what's up, Willard?" Longarm said.

Allred glanced around as though he might be overheard, then in a husky whisper said, "Last night I kinda did a drunken crawl from saloon to saloon, down in the worst part of the Acre."

"Find Quincy Ballentine?"

Allred's face lit up in a radiant smile. "Nope, but I found one of his bully boys."

Chapter 11

A steady stream of Fort Worth locals, dust-covered trail hands, traveling gamblers, whiskey drummers, fancy dressed ladies of questionable occupation, uniformed soldiers, and bleary-eyed railroaders continued to move around Longarm and Willard Allred, who stood rooted to their spots in the middle of Third Street.

Longarm perked up considerably, then said, "Who and where?"

"The one and only Dead Eyed Zeke Cobb. He's been holed up for a day or two playin' poker in a rougher'n-a-wood-rasp joint called the Gilded Lily. It's way down on Front Street and Rusk, not far from the Texas and Pacific Depot. One of the first saloons ever built in Fort Worth. Scruffy waterin' hole ain't exactly in hell, but any man what steps outta the Lily's batwing doors can see the fiery pit and smell the brimstone from its south-facin' veranda."

"Couldn't find Quincy, huh?"

"Sorry, Marshal. Nothin' firm on the man's where-abouts as yet. But if'n anyone knows where ole Quincy is, I'd bet on Cobb."

"He still at his cards?"

"Yep. Leastways he was when I left there less than half an hour ago. And he's been drinkin' pretty heavy, as well. Losin' and drinkin'. Ain't a real good combination."

Longarm glanced up and down the busy street, then scratched his chin. An unescorted but fetching blue-eyed woman, her blond hair set off by a tiny, wine-colored, wedge-shaped hat, offered up a coquettish smile when he tipped his Stetson as she passed. Most likely a demi-monde, Longarm thought. Shouldn't be on the street un-accompanied anyway.

"Think I'll go to the room and fetch my shotgun to take along 'fore we brace 'im," Longarm said.

"Already done 'er. Big popper's under the seat of the wagon."

"Well, then, Deputy Willard, let's go on down there and throw a net over the skunk, then shake him till his teeth rattle. Ole Zeke's way overdue for a come-to-Jesus meetin'. And I'm just the man to lead the hymn singin' and tithe collectin' at his soul savin'."

On the south side of Front Street, at the corner of Rusk, Tater Allred reined his team to a stop less than thirty minutes later. Without speaking, he nodded toward a primitive, square, squatty, board-and-batten building. A badly faded sign hung over the sloped veranda's roof. Visitors standing in the street could now barely make out the name—once painted on the facade in vivid reds and bright yellows—even in the dazzling Texas sunlight of midday.

The Gilded Lily looked to Longarm like everything that exemplified the exact opposite of the White Ele-phant. Half the size of Luke Short's glorious drinking and gambling establishment, this scruffy, cow-country "oasis" had seen much better days. And though he tried, Longarm couldn't imagine how far back in the past those days might have been.

Almost a dozen tired-looking cow ponies, arranged in two groups of five or six, stood hipshot at the hitching posts on either side of the saloon's hard-used front entrance. A plate glass window made up most of the wall on the right side of the off-kilter batwing doors. An extended lack of attention to anything like cleanliness made it virtually impossible to see any of the action going on inside.

Squint-eyed, Longarm surveyed every crack and nail head of the disreputable establishment before making a move. After nearly a minute of careful scrutiny, he climbed down from Allred's well-used wagon, then reached into the box and slid his sawed-off Greener from beneath the seat.

Tater brought his Yellow Boy Winchester out and followed Longarm. He hovered near the marshal's left elbow, like a baby chick being escorted by a mother hen, as they strolled across the empty street.

The lawmen stepped up on the Gilded Lily's warped-plank porch about the same time several cowboys stumbled from inside through the swinging doors. Someone in the rowdy group laughed, another whooped and shouted. A third leather pounder cut loose with a string of unintelligible epithets at anything handy—his horse, an uncooperative chippy, a surly bartender, and the uncommon prevalence "of cheap, rot-gut whiskey in Fort Worth's Hell's Half Acre."

Two men in the disorderly group got into a loud argument over who'd fucked the ugliest whore. The others pulled them apart. Then the entire party finally headed for their tough-looking little cow ponies, saddled up, and rode north along Rusk Street like a cloud of rolling thunder, punctuated by firing their pistols into the air.

Longarm propped his big-bore Greener against a porch pillar, pulled out two nickel cheroots, and handed one of them to his brand-new special deputy. Once they got lit up, he said, "Tell me what the inside of this place looks like, Tater. Give me as complete a layout as you can, and say where you saw Cobb seated when last you were here."

"Well, Marshal, the Lily ain't nothin' more'n a single oblong room. When we step inside, the bar, what there is of it, is on the right. Stretches from a few feet past the window yonder and runs almost all the way to the back wall. Six or eight tables along the left for them as want to drink. Area at the back is for gamblin'."

Longarm gave the information careful thought, glanced at the dram shop's batwing doors, then nodded.

Motioning with his cigar, Willard said, "Zeke's a-sittin' at the farthest table from the entrance, right in the back corner not far from the only exit on that end of the buildin'. Tell the truth, Marshal Long, might be somewhat problematic to get at 'im, 'less maybe we can surprise the evil bastard."

Longarm snatched his ten-gauge blaster up, broke it open, and checked the brass-jacketed shells inside. He snapped the gun shut with a loud click, lowered the weapon's muzzle, and pressed it against his leg, then said, "Well, Tater, why don't we just stroll on in and see what's happening. Maybe we can surprise ole Zeke."

A dense, wall-like cloud of smoke, from nigh fifty different kinds of twisted tobacco, wafted though the room on the stuffy interior air. It made it difficult to see in the dimly lit joint. Almost every table had six or eight cowboys crowded around, puffing away as they played poker, drank, or just enjoyed the society of their fellows. Several desperately haggard, rough-looking women apathetically shuffled from one table to the next, made halfhearted efforts to interest one man or another, then moved on.

Longarm made his way down the entire length of a coarse bar that consisted of little more than one-by-twelve rough-cut, pine planks sitting atop a series of empty whiskey barrels. Here and there, battered spittoons decorated with splattered gobs of greasy spittle occupied easy-to-hit spots. But even a perfunctory examination of the filthy floor revealed that most men didn't bother much with their aim when it came time to cut loose.

Longarm stopped at the corner of the crude counter farthest from the door and stared at the empty poker table in the corner. "Looks like we musta missed him, Tater."

The words had barely fallen from his lips when a toothless crone, who could have easily been Longarm's grandmother, pushed her way into his face and grabbed his crotch. In something close to a nightmarish screech, she yelped, "Goddamn, but you are one big, good-lookin' sumbitch. Ain't seen nothin' like you 'round here in more'n a year. Bet you'd give a gal one helluva romp."

Longarm made a bit more than a halfhearted effort to push the woman away, but couldn't break her talon-like grip on his cock. "Sorry, miss, uh ma'am, uh madam, uh granny, but this just ain't the right time."

"Granny? Come on, honey. I'll show you what ole Granny can do. Plenty a empty rooms out back. Just walk me through 'at 'ere door over yonder, and in ten minutes I'll suck on this big ole wanger of yer'n till your Stetson caves in flatter'n a cow flop. Won't cost you but two dollars. Whatta ya say, big boy?"

Willard said, "Get away, Mabel."

The woman ignored him. She snatched out the top portion of her false teeth, made a disgusting slurping noise, then said, "How 'bout a dollar, honey. Garn-damn-tee it'll be the best blow job you've ever had. Ole Mabel's known from Amarillo to Laredo, from Longview to El Paso for her ability to suck the bluin' off'n a rifle barrel."

In spite of his discomfort with the hag's sour-smelling proximity, an uneasy, slightly amused smile split Longarm's face. "Now you know that's one hell of an offer, miss, I mean ma'am, or whatever. But I'm afraid I can't accommodate you right at the moment. Have other far more important business to conduct, you see."

Willard grabbed the woman by the elbow, pulled her around to face him, then said, "Go on now, Mabel. Put your damned teeth back in. Give it a rest. Get away from here. This man don't want nothin' you're a-sellin'. Take your scrawny old ass on back to the cow chasers and leave 'im be."

The ancient whore flashed both men a hellish, gummy smile, and finally released her viselike grip on Longarm's equipment. She ran a snaky tongue across still empty gums, poked Longarm in the chest with a knob-knuckled, witchy finger, then said, "Now that's really too bad, honey. You don't know what you're a-missin'. Two bucks ain't nothin' for the kinda blow job I can give you. Might as well be givin' it away, for a measly fuckin' buck."

"Tell your story a-walkin', Mabel," Allred snapped.

The ancient whore slapped her teeth back in her

118

mouth, wrestled them into place, then said, "Need to stop listnin' to old farts like Willard, mister. He ain't been able to get it up since the Big War ended back in sixty-five." She cackled like one of Satan's imps, staggered back into the swirling bank of tobacco smoke, and disappeared as quickly as she'd first materialized.

Allred watched until the most hideous mattress back in Hell's Half Acre vanished. Then he motioned to a short, rat-faced bartender, who sported a greasy head of thinning black hair and a moustache the size of a trail cook's camp skillet. The drink slinger hustled over as quickly as a gimpy, dragging foot would allow. He snapped a nasty rag at some trash and a pile of dead flies on the bar, then cast darting, edgy glances at his new customers.

"What's up, Tater?" the bartender said.

Allred cast guarded glances around the room, then, under his breath, said, "Louis Boucher, this here gent's Deputy U.S. Marshal Custis Long. I'm here as his specially appointed deputy. We're a-lookin' for Zeke Cobb. I seen ole Zeke in here a-sittin' at that table yonder, my very own self, not more'n a hour ago."

Boucher leaned forward. He spoke as though telling a well-kept and dangerous-to-know secret. "Fellers a-playin' poker at that table took a break. All of 'em should be back soon. They've been a-goin' at it now for almost two days. Some of 'em is gettin' kinda wore down. Heard Cobb say he's gonna have a bite to eat, then be on back shortly."

Longarm cast a quick glance at the empty table. All the chairs were leaned forward to discourage anyone from attempting to sit. "Any reason to believe he might not return, Mr. Boucher?" he asked.

119

Boucher shook his head. "None a'tall. I done been waitin' that table damn near the whole time. Zeke's a big loser in the game. Wants to get some of his money back, I'd imagine. The stupid son of a bitch cain't play cards for spit, but he hates to lose worse'n anybody I've ever seen."

Longarm did another quick assessment of the busy saloon, then turned back to Boucher. "Tell you what, Louis. I think me and Willard will stake out a claim to this corner of the bar and wait. Zeke don't know either of us. Leastways, don't believe he does. Anyway, we'll take him down, then move him out through the back door as quickly and quietly as we can. Rest of your payin' customers shouldn't even know anything's happenin'."

Boucher arched an eyebrow, tilted his head like an inquisitive dog, then said, "Gonna look forward to seein' that trick. Have to take the man by surprise. He won't go any other way. Hell, ole Zeke don't do nothin' 'less he wants to. You boys best be prepared for trouble aplenty."

"Ain't no big problem, Louis. We can whack him across the noggin with a gun barrel, then drag his ass out the back door," Allred said. "Hell, he's damn near a-sittin' in the door as it is. Won't have to haul him more'n a dozen steps to the alley and away from everyone else."

A crooked grin creaked across Boucher's deeply lined face. "Yeah, if'n you can get close enough to pull it off. 'Course, he just might gun down both of you 'fore you're able to get within ten feet." He slapped at the splinter-laden countertop with his rag again and said, "You boys want anything? Might look better if'n you got somethin' in front of you."

Longarm and Allred loitered at the end of the bar and

nursed their drinks for nearly an hour before the poker klatch at the back table finally began to regroup. Dead Eyed Zeke Cobb was the last participant to show up. Willard elbowed Longarm, who had the spot nearest the gathering, and pointed with a single finger. The inebriated outlaw wobbled into the room and headed for the game.

Dead Eyed Zeke Cobb was the size of a grizzly. A ragged suit coat worn over a brown, collarless shirt added to the image of a prowling animal. His right eye had no color. An ugly slash mark of angry, pink flesh ran from a butchered brow, down the man's cheek, and disappeared into his thick, unkempt beard.

In a coarse whisper, Longarm said, "If he passes close enough, I'll jump the evil fucker. We'll play it exactly the way you described. Put him down quick, then get him the hell outta here, fast as we can."

"Lead the way, Marshal. I'm right behind you."

Cobb's drunken state appeared to require most of his concentration. He took no notice of anyone, shouldered his way past several cowboys, then staggered by the far corner of the bar. Had his back turned when Longarm stepped forward, brought the ten-gauge Greener up, and swung it like a club. The weapon's heavy barrel came down atop Cobb's tall-crowned Texas hat and knocked the man forward by two stumbling steps.

To Longarm's utter surprise, Cobb stayed erect. The outlaw turned, felt the crushed crown of his hat, and said, "What the fuck . . ." Then growled like an angry bear and went for the pistol laid across his belly.

Longarm swatted at Cobb's gun hand with the shotgun's stock. He knocked the pistol to one side. The weapon went off with a thunderous explosion. The shot blew a hole in the poker table, scattering chips, cards, and wood splinters into the air like blowing leaves.

Willard Allred darted past Longarm, brought his Yellow Boy Winchester's barrel around, and whacked their prey across the back of the neck. Cobb's only good eye flipped up into the back of his skull. For a second, he swayed like a tree in a stiff wind, then went to ground like a sack full of horseshoes dropped from a plow-pusher's hayloft.

Longarm grabbed one arm, Willard the other. In a matter of seconds, Dead Eyed Zeke Cobb lay stretched out in the stinking garbage- and filth-littered alleyway behind the Gilded Lily. "Well, Tater, man's head must be harder'n the hubs of hell. Thought I whacked him pretty good. Barrel of my Greener didn't even seem to have any effect a'tall."

Allred gazed down into Cobb's face. "Big ole hat of his cushioned the blow, Marshal Long. Learned when I was in prison, you gotta hit a man wearin' a hat that big 'cross the back of the neck. Blow'll put 'im down in a heartbeat."

Louis Boucher burst through the Lily's back door and eased up to Cobb's prone figure. He stood over the outlaw and twisted his bar rag into a knot. "Dead?"

Longarm leaned against a stack of empty freight crates. "Nope. Still very much alive, Louis." He propped the shotgun against his leg, pulled out a fresh cheroot, and lit it. As he shook the match out, he said, "We'll wait till he comes around, talk to him a spell, then fetch his sorry ass down to Sam Farmer's jail. Lock him away for a spell."

A puzzled look flashed across Boucher's pinched face. "You gonna question him out here in the alley?"

"That's the plan," Longarm said.

The Gilded Lily's bartender pointed to a spot deeper into the alleyway. "Can you take 'im back yonder behind them boxes and barrels and stuff? That way any of our customers as comes out here to relieve themselves won't see what's goin' on."

"Understand completely, Louis," Longarm said. "We'll move him out of the way. Wouldn't want to offend any drunk forced to take a piss out here while we're beatin' the hell out of ole Dead Eyed Zeke."

Chapter 12

Longarm propped Zeke Cobb against the bottom barrel in a stack of empties that had once held whiskey shipped across the Atlantic from Scotland. He squatted in front of the unconscious brigand, then slapped him across the mouth several times.

Willard Allred stood to one side near Cobb's feet. He held Longarm's shotgun leveled at the outlaw's guts and appeared anxious to use it.

"Come on, you son of a bitch. Wake up. Got some important questions for you." Longarm slapped the man again. Harder. Then again. Harder still. He grabbed the front of Cobb's coat with both hands, shook him, then slapped him a third time, then a fourth.

Cobb groaned. His eyes fluttered open. Shaking hands darted out in front of his face to fend off the blows. "Stop a-slappin' on me, you stupid bastard. Christ Almighty, I'm awake. Swear to Jesus. Can hear every word you're a-sayin'. What the fuck you want?"

Longarm stood, flicked a chewed cheroot away, then fished a fresh one from his vest pocket. He shoved the square-cut cigar into his mouth, then rolled it to one corner with his tongue. "I'm Deputy U.S. Marshal Custis Long, Zeke. This here's my specially appointed deputy Willard Allred. Sit up and pay attention. We've got questions you need to answer."

Cobb cut a nervous glance from Longarm to Allred. He shook a finger at Willard. "I've seen you afore. Hire out a run-down piece of a wagon. Seen you a-cartin' folks 'round town. Sure as hell didn't know you was no lawman."

Longarm snapped, "Look at me, Zeke. Try to get focused. We'll start with an easy one. Where's your boss, Quincy Ballentine?"

"Who?"

Longarm kicked Cobb in the side—just hard enough to get the man's painful, undivided attention. "Best start answerin' my questions, Cobb. I ain't inclined to spend a lot of my time messin' around with trash like you. Now put that lubricated-with-shit thinker mechanism of yours to work. Make it spit me out an answer I can use."

Cobb shook his head as though trying to remove water from his ears, or cobwebs from his brain. He grunted, then said, "Shit. Done went and forgot. Tell me again. What was the question?"

Longarm kicked him again. The air rushed from Cobb's lungs. He doubled over and grabbed himself around the middle with both arms. What little a person could see of his face turned scarlet with pain.

"Damn, but you are one stupid son of a bitch, Zeke. My leg's gettin' tired. But I'm here to tell you, this process is gonna get one helluva lot more brutal if you don't come up with a real good answer, and damned quick."

Cobb's only good eye darted from one of his tormentors' faces to the other, as though he expected to find some small degree of sympathy. "You cain't do this, goddammit. This ain't no civilized kinda treatment. Cain't just go a-kickin' the hell out of a man like this. What the hell kinda marshals are you? Jesus, beatin' on a man like this ain't lawful. 'Sides that, it just ain't right."

Longarm snatched the cheroot out of his mouth, bent down with the cigar between his fingers, then shook it in Cobb's face. "Well, when we get through here, we'll run you up to the north end of town. You can stand beside Matilda Wayland's bed. If she's conscious and her ears ain't swollen so bad she can't hear, you can tell her all about how it's just not *lawful* to go and treat bad-assed bastards like you with anything but kid gloves."

Willard stepped around to Cobb's opposite side and kicked him from a new direction. The milky-eyed villain yelped like a surprised dog. He grabbed his gut again and squealed, "Fuckin' shit. Okay. Okay. Whatta ya wanna know? Jus' ask me again. Swear I'll tell whatever I can, if'n I know."

Longarm squatted and got as close to the man as he dared. His face twisted into a grimace, then he said, "Jesus, Cobb, you smell like a wet cow flop. Don't you ever even wipe your nasty ass?"

Cobb looked puzzled. "That one of them questions you want answered?"

"Jesus," Longarm spat. "Where's Quincy Ballentine, you idiot?"

Cobb groaned. "Swear 'fore Jesus, Marshal, I don't know."

Longarm glanced up at Allred. A flicked finger was all it took. Another kick landed in the same spot as the one before it, only harder the second time. Cobb rolled onto his side and drew up into a tight, coughing knot in an effort to protect himself. He whimpered, snorted into his stinking, piss-saturated dirt, then rolled onto his stomach with his face inside his hat.

Longarm could barely hear Cobb when he said, "Sweet Merciful Mother of God. Damnation. I'm a-tellin' you true, so far as I'm aware of it. You can kick me all you want, I guess, but I cain't tell you where Quincy is, right now. Man cain't tell what he don't know. Only person as might possibly be able to point you in the right direction is Silas."

"Silas Brakett?" Allred shot back.

Cobb rolled onto his back. He scrambled to his knees, then crawled to the barrel and leaned against it. His head came up just enough to be better heard. "Who the fuck else, you ugly piece of rebel trash! I don't travel with no Silas Jones, or Silas Smith, or Silas Williams. Christ, please save me from Southern stupidity. Ain't never knowed a lawman, or a reb, yet what possessed any more brains than a rabid possum. All you Southern ones is even stupider."

"Well, that's just all fine and dandy, Zeke," Longarm snorted. "But where in the blue-eyed hell's Silas? You gonna tell us, or do we have to get real serious about kickin' the dog shit outta you? Bet if we both really concentrate on the effort at the same time, we could literally stomp the hell outta you in a matter of a few minutes. Both us ole *Southern* boys just might take all our former frustrations over losin' the *Big War* out on your sorry ass."

"Look, I'm a-tellin' you, ain't no need to go kickin' on me, or whackin' me in the head again, or anything else like that. 'Cause no matter how much you do it, ain't gonna get you any different answer. I don't know where Quincy is."

Willard grinned. "Think you forgot the most recent question, asshole. We believe you about Quincy. Where's Silas?"

Cobb wagged his head like a tired dog. "Last I heard he wuz shacked up in Lou Brown's parlor house. Lou's got a pair of straw-haired twins a-workin' for her that Silas favors. He tole me them girls has that same kind of hair on they pussies. Says them girls got the softest hair on they crotches he done ever felt in his entire life. Like pettin' a cat. Must really be somethin' to see up close, I suppose. Honest to God, Marshal, that's all I know. Cain't help you no more'n that."

Longarm glanced at Allred. "You familiar with the place, Willard?"

"Sure. Lou owned the old Waco Tap Saloon 'fore it burnt slap to the ground. She moved into a good-sized place at about Eighth and Calhoun, not far from the still-smokin' Tap's ashes, and opened a rip-snorter of a whorehouse almost as rough as her saloon."

"Most parlor houses tend to attract a better-heeled crowd, Willard."

"Yeah, well, Lou's joint ain't what anybody'd call an honest-to-God, real fancy dancy parlor house. That's for damned sure. Joint's rough as a petrified corn cob. Has a big ole room up front that's large enough for cowboys to visit with the girls, or dance, if'n they've a mind."

"So, it's a *combination* dance hall and brothel."

Willard propped the heavy shotgun across his arm. "Kinda. More like a gussied-up hog ranch, if'n you ask me. But the place does have its positives. Lou keeps a three-piece band—pianner, trumpet, and banjo—for the dancin' at night. Whole backside of the place is chopped up into eight or ten private rooms where the working girls can conduct their *business*."

"Busy?"

"Oh, yeah. 'Course, I don't think there's more'n five or six girls workin' at any one time. Cowboys what show up at Lou's place got plenty of choices about where they wanna flop and what they can get for their money."

"Sounds like a great joint," Longarm snorted.

"It's the roughest bagnio in Hell's Half Acre, Marshal Long. Hear tell as how more cowboys've lit a shuck for the Pearly Gates in Lou Brown's joint than in any other bordello in the Acre. A man can get dead mighty quick over there. No tellin' what we might come up against in her place. Not the least of a man's worries is Lou. Hear tell that big ole gal's dispatched at least three fellers her very own self."

Longarm turned his attention back to Cobb. "Does Silas have a favorite girl at Brown's that he especially likes, Zeke?"

Cobb rubbed his ribs. "Done tole you 'bout them twins."

"I know, but is there anyone else?"

"Oh. They's a big-tittied gal called Nellie Belle Squires, as I jus' come to remember. He done tole me as how that woman can fuck like an Arizona mountain lion with its ass on fire. 'Course I wouldn't be a-knowing nothin' 'bout fuckin' no wild animals, but if anyone would do such an unnatural act, it'd be Silas."

Head cocked to one side, Willard said, "How's that, Zeke?"

"Well, reb, rumors have it as how Silas wuz raised by wolves. Then they's the story goin' 'round as how he got

130

cotched a-fuckin' a goat when he wuz a-growin' up on the farm. Know he's real touchy if'n you mention anythang like that. And, as my ole white-haired granddaddy liked to say, the man's lock nut 'pears to have been cross threaded right smart." Cobb crawled to his knees, came painfully to his feet, then leaned against the barrel like he might fall down again. "His head's a damn site smaller'n his hat—'cause of a serious lack of brains, you know."

"He's crazy?" Longarm snorted.

"Well, let's just say he's about a number three grain scoop short on anything like smarts. Hear tell a horse kicked him in the head when he wuz a nubbin. Might explain a nasty scar on his forehead just above the eye. But don't underestimate 'im. Son of a bitch scares the bejabbers outta me."

The news of Silas Brakett's scary lunacy came as something of a surprise to both Longarm and Willard Allred. Brakett carried a hard-earned reputation as a badman, but neither of the lawmen had ever heard of any insanity.

"Nothin' worse'n tryin' to corral a lunatic," Longarm muttered. "Go get the wagon, Tater. Bring it 'round front of the Lily. I'll meet you there."

Willard started away, then turned back. "What you gonna be doin'?"

"Need to speak with Zeke in private for a minute. Don't worry, I'll be right along."

Longarm watched Allred until he disappeared around the corner of the saloon's front facade, then got right up in Cobb's face. "Here's the deal, Zeke. You're gonna get on your horse and get the hell outta Fort Worth soon's I'm gone. Don't even look back. Ride

131

hard till you're in Austin, or go to El Paso. Hell, go to Amarillo if'n you've a mind. Whatever you do, don't let me see your face again while I'm here."

Cobb's faced reddened. "By God, you got no paper on me. Cain't go a-runnin' me outta town like a fuckin' animal. I ain't done a single thing what would warrant you a-treatin' me like this."

Their hat brims touched when Longarm snarled, "Don't let me see your face again, you stupid son of a bitch. I'll come shootin' next time we meet on the streets of Hell's Half Acre. As God is my witness, I swear it."

Chapter 13

Lou Brown's parlor house looked just a bit out of place for Hell's Half Acre. For all a casual passing observer could tell, the busy whorehouse could have easily been the residence of a bespectacled old maid schoolteacher. A white picket fence surrounded the famed madam's large yard. A deep layer of well-kept green grass framed a variety of colorful flowers that decorated either side of the gravel walk. A brightly painted, deep, covered veranda spread across the entire front of the house and appeared to serve as an overflow waiting area for gathering customers.

Willard Allred pulled his wagon to a stop at the end of the walkway, climbed down, then looped the leather reins through a brass ring held by the hand of one of at least a dozen painted metal jockeys that stood like grinning guards in the place of hitch rails. "Place don't look real busy at the moment, does it?"

Longarm stopped at the front gate long enough to run an inquisitive gaze from one side of the building to the other. "Yep. Looks right peaceful, don't it? Can't see but three horses out here, right now. For sure everything will heat up soon as the sun goes down."

Willard nodded, checked the loads in the shotgun again, then mumbled, "Oh, she'll heat up alright. 'Fore the night's over, there'll be fifty or sixty cowboys go through this place. Lucky ones will get out alive and go on to Dodge or wherever else they're headed. Lou's gals gonna get another heavy-duty workout."

Longarm pushed the gate open, ambled up the gravel walk, then climbed the steps onto Lou Brown's closed-at-the-bottom, open-at-the-top porch. Cane-bottomed chairs lined the outside front wall of the house. Slat-backed swings hung from chains on either side of the entrance.

Allred pointed to a brass chain dangling from a hole in the door frame and said, "Have to ring the bell. Lou's got a thing about folks a-beatin' on her door. She won't even bother to answer till a body pulls on that piece of chain."

"Ah, wouldn't want to do anything to upset the lady now, would we?" Longarm said as he jerked on the bell ringer.

"And Marshal," Allred added, "be careful of Lou. She's hell on wheels in a fight. Heard one tale as how she damn near beat one of Marshal Farmer's policemen to death with a sawed-off pool cue. Keeps one hangin' from a leather strap somewheres under her dress. Woman's also been known to carry a big ole bowie knife and a four-barreled derringer."

"Well, Jesus, Willard, that's mighty comfortin'. Wish you'd mentioned some of the lady's more violent proclivities 'fore we got over here."

Longarm jerked the chain, then stood away from the screen. For several seconds he heard the thumping, bumping sounds of people scurrying around inside. The glass-paned portal popped open to reveal a tall, stately, ample bosomed, auburn-haired woman wearing a black dress that fell to the floor in a cascade of fancy, stiff ruffles. Heavily rouged and dipped in a powerful perfume that oozed through the screened door and assaulted Longarm's nose, the moose-sized madam pushed the screen open and motioned them inside.

As they eased past her, Lou Brown cast a narrow glance at each man, then said, "Who's your friend, Tater? Has the look of a man who could ride the tiger all night long. Got some mighty fine-lookin' gals here at Lou's just a-waitin' fer fellers like you to show up, mister. All you gotta do is name your favorite fantasy. My girls are experienced. They're here to fulfill your every wish and desire. So, what'll it be? Just name your pleasure."

Longarm slipped his silver deputy marshal's star from his vest pocket and flipped its leather holder open. "Actually, Miss Brown, we're here on official business."

Lou Brown's face flushed. "That's Mrs. Brown to you, you badge-totin' cocksucker." The moose-sized madam had the kind of voice that got inside a man's head and felt like it was scratching on the back of his eyeballs.

Longarm leaned away from the verbal blast. "No need to get all worked up, Mrs. Brown."

Four half-dressed girls bounded from a hallway in the center of the wall across the back of the large entry room. Their employer waved them off with a spangle-covered, ebony-colored feather she held in one hand. "Get back inside, goddammit. This bastard's just another law pusher lookin' for a freebie." The surprised women collided with one another like a derailed freight train, then turned and, giggling like children, hustled back in the direction from which they'd just come.

135

Longarm shoved the leather wallet holding the badge back into his pocket, then removed his hat. He smiled and attempted a pleasant demeanor. "No need to get belligerent, Mrs. Brown. Can assure you, we're not here to shake you down, or take undue advantage in any way whatsoever."

The stout madam socked balled fists onto generous hips, leaned toward the object of her red-cheeked ire, and shot back, "Well, now, that'd be a first, if'n I ever heard of one. I've been working the pussy game for nigh on thirty years, Mr. Marshal."

"Long, ma'am. Marshal Custis Long."

"If you ain't here for a com-pli-mentary round of the old slap and tickle, Marshal Custis Long, you'd be the first I've ever encountered in all my years of seeing to the needs of workin' girls."

Willard Allred moved to a spot closer to Longarm, then said, "He's tellin' the truth, Lou. We're here on official business."

The formidable Mrs. Brown appeared to relax a bit. "What kind of official business, Tater? Every time I hear that phrase, it usually means I'm gonna have to fork up another bag full of money to keep the law outta my hair."

Longarm touched Allred on the sleeve. "We believe a man named Silas Brakett might be visiting with some of your girls. Perhaps the twins."

"The twins? You mean the Preston girls? Lily and Lucy?"

"Are the Preston girls twins?"

"Well, yes. Only set in the house."

"Would bet Lily and Lucy Preston are exactly who we're lookin' for, ma'am. Didn't see any blond-haired duplicates with the group who greeted us when we came in. Could the Preston girls possibly be in the company of Brakett at this very moment?"

Instead of answering the question, Lou Brown snapped, "Whaddaya want with Silas Brakett?"

"Then you do know the man?"

"Of course, I know Silas. He usually stops by for a visit every time he's in town. One of our most frequent customers, as a matter of pure fact." All of a sudden, Mrs. Brown's face reddened again. She shook a finger at Longarm. "And I don't like the fact that you're here to disrupt my operation by botherin' a well-paying, frequent customer."

Allred held up a peacemaking hand. "Just wanna talk with 'im for a few minutes, Lou. Have some important questions for the man. Soon's he answers 'em, we'll be gone."

For several tense seconds, Mrs. Brown tapped her foot and studied her tormentors as though she might snatch their heads off and then pitch the rendered, blood-squirting noggins into her front yard like so much garbage.

Finally, the angry madam toed at the tattered rug beneath her feet, then pointed at the doorway where the first four girls had disappeared. "Down the hall, all the way to the end. Last door on the left. Can't miss it. Silas has been in there ever since yesterday afternoon. Says he plans to stay at least one more night. Hope he does. Man always pays in gold."

Longarm nodded, placed his hat against his chest, and offered the woman an abbreviated cavalier's chivalrous bow. "Office of the U.S. marshal's service appreciates your cooperation, Mrs. Brown. Promise we'll do our very best not to disrupt your business operations any more than absolutely necessary."

"Well, I certainly hope the fuck you're a man of your word, Marshal Long. Whatever you have to do, do it quick, and then get the hell out," Lou Brown snorted, then stomped across the room and disappeared through a door in the farthest corner of the room.

Behind a cupped palm, Willard whispered, "Them's her *private quarters*. Ain't met anyone yet as has ever even been inside that part of the house."

Longarm stuffed his hat on, mumbled, "Of course," then headed for the open door to the whorehouse's hall. As he crossed the threshold, he slipped his pistol from its cross-draw holster and cocked it. Willard followed, shotgun in hand.

They tiptoed down the cramped hallway and stopped on either side of the room Lou Brown had indicated. A rough wooden sign painted with red hearts, white lace, and pink-cheeked cherubs was emblazoned with the single word TWINS.

Longarm pushed the brim of his hat up, then pressed an ear against the door. After several seconds, he stood and whispered, "Not a sound. Maybe they're all asleep."

Allred hissed, "Could be. If he's got his pants off and snoozin', whole dance should go a lot easier for us."

Longarm stepped back and lifted a leg to kick the door open. He thought better of the action, stepped back up to the portal and turned the knob. The door popped open and swung noiselessly toward the wall.

The overpowering musk of raw, squirting sex, combined with the body odor of several people, whiskey-saturated bedding, stale tobacco smoke, and the contents of a chamber pot hidden somewhere under the rumpled bed, slapped Longarm and Willard in their faces like someone had swatted them across the cheeks with the wet leather glove of a working buffalo hunter. The entire room looked brown, even the sheets on the bed.

On the far side of the sparsely furnished space, an iron-framed bed stood against the wall. Atop twisted sheets and a variety of other bedraggled bedding lay three sweat-drenched, spooned-up naked bodies. Lying between the Preston sisters, Silas Brakett appeared to still have his dick inside the fair-skinned girl closest to the wall. He gently hunched the girl from behind, even as he snorted and snored away like the big blade in a sawmill ripping its way through an oak log.

Longarm eased into the room, then took two quick steps that placed him right beside the bed. In short order, Willard took a spot at the end of the bed and leveled the shotgun on Brakett's sleeping figure.

The girl on the side of the bed nearest Longarm opened her pale blue eyes. She made no effort to cover her nude body. Ruby lips parted as though she might speak, just as he placed a finger over them, shook his head, and hissed, "Sssssh. Quiet, darlin'. Now, come on outta there."

Longram took the naked girl by the hand. With great care and deliberateness, she swung one shapely leg, then the other, over the mattress's edge, then stood. Her heavy breasts pressed against his chest. She smiled, then twisted back and forth, rubbing dark, thumb-sized nipples across his vest front until they stiffened to the point where he could actually feel them through his clothing.

An inquisitive hand came up to his crotch and squeezed. She leaned forward till her lips touched his ear.

"Uhmmmm. You're a big ole boy," she whispered. "Good-lookin' one, too. Even smell good. Don't get many like you in here, mister. You finish up with whatever you're here for, me and Lily'll fuck you till you cain't climb on a horse. Be so weak when you leave, your friend at the foot of the bed'll have to help you walk."

Longarm whispered back, "Might be gunplay in here soon, miss. Best get your sister up and get the hell out. 'Less you don't mind flyin' lead and the possibility of dyin' in this nasty fuckin' room."

Lucy Preston's head popped back, then she twisted and gazed down at her sister. As if by magic, the other naked girl stirred, then rose on one elbow and gazed around the room as though not the least surprised, or concerned, by the fact that two more men had entered. She carefully extracted herself from Silas Brakett's rigid manhood, then crawled to the foot of the bed. Brakett grunted and rolled onto his back, his thick, rock-hard cock pointing toward the ceiling like a fleshy flagpole.

Allred urged the girl toward her duplicate, who stood beside Longarm with her arms out. The girls hugged each other, then, without another sound, disappeared into the hallway.

Longarm watched until convinced the women were safe, then turned his attention back to the brigand in the bed. He tapped Brakett on the shoulder with the barrel of his pistol and waited—nothing. He tried again— nothing. On the third attempt to awaken the snoring slug, Brakett grunted, then swatted at the irritant. He scratched his crotch, stroked his stiff prong several times, and then, to Longarm's surprise, the man went at himself with considerable devotion.

"Well, by God, that's enough," Longarm said aloud.

He glanced at Willard Allred. A toothy grin creaked across the old soldier's face.

"Appears the man cain't git enough."

Longarm shook his head in disgust. "Tell you, Willard, I'll do a lot of things in service of the law, but I ain't gonna stand here and watch this bastard jerk off like a thirteen-year-old who's only recently discovered how good his damned pecker feels." He swung the Frontier model pistol barrel around and knocked Brakett's dick out of the sleeping man's fist. The outlaw let out a screech and sat bolt upright in the bed. Both hands dove to cover his wounded prong.

Chapter 14

Silas Brakett's ratlike eyes fluttered open. For several seconds they continued to flap like a covey of south Texas quail rising from scrub mesquite. He shook his head as though trying to clear out a skull full of cobwebs. "Sweet Jesus. Who're you two assholes, and whattaya want, for Christ's sake?"

He glanced down at the hands covering his damaged prick. A stream of bright red blood oozed up between trembling fingers. His startled gaze shot back up to Longarm. "God Almighty. My dick's a-bleedin'. What the fuck did you do to me? Oh Christ, I'm afraid to look. You ain't gone and cut ole Big Boy off, did you?"

Longarm smiled. "Hell, you'll be fine, Silas. Guess the blade sight on my pistol barrel musta put a nail-sized nick in that little bitty thang of yours."

A confused, dumbfounded look darted across Brakett's stubble-covered face. "Blade sight? Pistol barrel? You mean you whacked me on my dingus with a pistol barrel? Jesus, why? What kinda evil son of a bitch'd do such a thing?"

Willard tapped the foot of the iron bed frame with

the barrel of his shotgun. "You wanna talk to him here, Marshal? Or would you rather he got up, got dressed, and we took him out in the alley and beat the hell out of 'im, like we did Zeke Cobb?"

"Marshal? You boys the law?"

"Deputy U.S. Marshal Custis Long. That's my special deputy, Willard Allred."

"What the fuck'd you star-totin' bastards do to poor ole Zeke?"

"Nothin' much," Longarm said. "Just asked him a few questions, then told him to get the hell outta town."

Brakett's gaze wobbled back down to his crotch. He opened bloody hands and cast an inquisitive gander at his wounded equipment. Then he shot an angry, teeth-gritting, hot-eyed glare at Longarm. "Jesus. Poor son of a bitch ain't gonna be no use to me for a good long spell, you stupid, law-bringin' cocksucker. Tell you what, you hand me my clothes and pistols off'n that chair yonder. Get myself dressed, we'll all go out in the street, an' I'll just kill the hell outta both your sorry asses."

Longarm cocked the Colt and leveled the muzzle at Brakett's damaged goods. "Any killin' you're gonna do'll have to wait. Right now you're gonna tell me where Quincy Ballentine is, or I'm gonna blow your balls off right where you're sittin'."

A twitching mask of alarm spread over Brakett's face. He covered himself again. "The hell you say. You wouldn't do such an awful thing to any man."

"He would," Willard snarled. "And if'n he won't, I sure as hell will."

Brakett's troubled, darting gaze swung around to Allred. He squinted in recognition. "Hell, I know you," he said. "You're that broke-down old reb what drives a freight wagon around town and calls it a hack. Seen you almost ever' day since we come to town. What the fuck're you doin' a-helpin' a federal lawdog?"

"This conversation is on the way to gettin' borin' as hell, and I'm somewhat less than inclined to take the time and explain *absolutely everything* to you, chapter and verse, unless I have to do it." Longarm pulled the trigger on his pistol. The gigantic .45 slug blasted a smoking hole in the mattress not two inches from Brakett's grasping fingers. The explosion, hemmed in by the closeness of the cramped room, was near deafening. The concussive shockwave from the blast snuffed out a lit kerosene lamp sitting atop a broken-down chest of drawers—the only other piece of furniture in the depressing, brown-hued room.

Eyes as big as dinner plates, Silas Brakett rubbed his ears with bloody fingers, then yelped, "He made a run up to Springtown. 'Bout twenty miles from here. Said he had to replace his favorite girl and knew a gal from up that way as he could put to work whorin' for 'im."

Longarm gritted his teeth. "Did he bother to mention what happened to his favorite girl?"

"Matilda?"

"Yes, you stupid bastard, Matilda."

"Well, yeah. Quincy tole me she quit 'im. Said she went on back to Dodge, where he found her in the first place. 'At gal wuz a-humpin' cowboys for a dollar a throw in a dirty-legged Kansas whorehouse when he come on her. Damn shame she went back, if'n you ask me. Matilda wuz, by far, the best-lookin', most high-toned woman he done ever had to keep him in walkin'-around money—and he's had some good'uns. I liked Matilda. Everyone what knowed her liked her. Damn good fuck, too, when you could catch her in the mood to let you rip off a little piece."

Longarm's eyes narrowed and one brow arched. "You mean Quincy's had other women who did the same kind of thing for him as Matilda?"

"'Course he has. Gets hisself a new one 'bout every other year or so."

A heavy silence hung over the room as the realization of what Brakett had just implied hit both lawmen. At the exact same moment, Longarm and Willard Allred both breathed, "Shit!"

Brakett shot a nervous glance from one man's face to the other. "What the hell's the difference? Cain't see how Quincy's keepin' company with one whore, or another, should matter to a federal lawdog and his half-assed special fuckin' deputy."

Willard Allred's face went red. He pushed past a surprised Longarm, swung the stock of the Greener around, and caught Brakett across the mouth. The blow knocked the brigand's head to one side, split both lips, and knocked out several teeth. A spray of blood shot onto Madam Lou Brown's bedroom wall and splattered like a fistful of thrown chicken guts.

A shocked screech bolted from Brakett's throat. He grabbed at his lower jaw with both hands, rolled onto his side, and passed out.

Willard drew back for another blow, but Longarm placed a quieting hand on the man's shoulder. "That's enough. He's out cold. Don't think you can hurt him much more'n you did, Willard, 'less maybe you want to shoot him a time or two."

Allred shook as though in the throes of a death-dealing case of malaria. His arms eased down to his sides and he quickly resumed his place at the end of the bed. "Sorry, Marshal," he said. "Didn't mean to lose my temper like that. But I gotta tell you, I'm sick to death of havin' scum like Silas Brakett treat me with a lot less than respect. Served my cause and fought with honor and distinction. I'll not have bastards like this one besmirch my service any longer. As of today I won't be takin' any more such bullshit off'n any of 'em."

"Understand completely, Willard. Trust me I do. But knocked colder'n a log-splitin' wedge in Montana, ole Silas there can't tell us a thing, and I need to know where Quincy's gonna be stayin' when he comes back from his recruitin' in Springtown. Understand?"

Still red-faced and shaking, Willard nodded. "Yessir. Understand completely. Guess I'd best go find some water, then try to bring him back around."

"Might be a good idea."

Willard hit the door running. A few minutes later he hustled back with a large ewer of fresh-pumped well water. He sat the pitcher on the floor, dipped a rag in the liquid, then laid it across Brakett's busted-up face.

Took some time and effort, but after about five minutes the still-naked thief and killer finally came around to bug-eyed consciousness. He picked at the empty spots in his mouth where teeth once resided, then said, "Wha fo' ya wen' an' hit me, you sommabitch? Shi', I wuz a-tryin' to tell ya' wha' ya' wanned ta know."

Longarm stared down at Brakett as though gazing into a pit of squirming snakes. He lifted the blood-spitting gunny's pistol belt off the battered chest and threw it over his shoulder. Not a scintilla of sympathy showed in the man's face when he said, "Get up and put your clothes on, Silas."

Brakett looked confused. "Wha' fo'?"

"Willard ran into Mrs. Brown out in the hall. She wants us all out of her house, and right 'by God' now. So, get up and get dressed."

Brakett struggled to the edge of the bed, leaving a trail of blood on the sheets behind him. "Guess my tim' wer' 'bout up, anaway. Only pay fo' las' nigh'." He threw spindly legs over the side of the lumpy, stained mattress and sat up. Longarm pitched him his pants, then his shirt, and finally a run-out pair of boots that barely had soles on them.

As Brakett tussled with his boots, Longarm said, "Tell me where Quincy's stayin'."

Still spitting blood and pieces of his teeth now and again, Brakett made a snorting sound, then glared at Longarm. "Yew mus' think I'm some kinda idget, or somefin'."

Willard pushed between the two men again, drew the shotgun's butt back, then snarled, "Tell the man what he wants to know, you stupid son of a bitch, or so help me God, you won't leave this room with a single tooth left in that empty head of yours when I get through beatin' on you . . ."

Longarm patted Allred on the shoulder and gently moved him aside. He casually leaned on the chest of drawers and rested his head in one hand, like a man bored beyond tears. "Look, Silas, I'm gonna tell you all about your present predicament. Quincy Ballentine damn near beat Matilda Wayland to death. Left her in an alley to die. Girl's laid up in bed as we speak, and could well pass in spite of a damned good doctor's best efforts. Now you're gonna tell me where you think Quincy'll be stayin' when he gets back to town, or I'm

gonna turn Willard loose to do whatever he feels necessary to get you to talk. You understand?"

Brakett stomped a reluctant foot into his boot, then
cast a beady-eyed glance at each man. As he sat on the
edge of the bed, his roving gaze lingered on Willard
Allred for a second, then went back to Longarm. "Yeah,
I unnerstan'. I don' tell, yew'll bea' me to death."

Longarm grinned. "Something like that. What it'll
all amount to is, if you don't talk, I'll let Willard do as
much damage to you as Quincy did to Matilda."

Brakett's eyes narrowed. A look of mild panic flitted
across his scarred face. "Arright, arright. Don' get
s'cited. They's a hotel down from the Comique call the
Drover's Inn. Rea' small place. Only ten room. On tha
corner a Eighth an' Throckmor'on Stree'. He's ga' two
rooms rented there. Should be back sometim' tamar-
rawer wid da new piece a twitsh."

"You sure about that?" Allred growled.

Brakett raised a hand as though testifying in court.
"All I know. Swear 'fore Jesus."

Longarm grabbed Willard by the elbow and urged
him into the hallway. "Meet me outside. Have a few
more words for our friend here, then I'll be right out."
Willard nodded and headed for the street.

Back inside the room, Longarm dumped the pistol
belt on the floor at the foot of the bed, then turned on
Brakett. "Tell you the same thing I told Cobb. Get out of
town. Get as far away from here as you can. Don't even
look back. If I see you here after today, I'll kill you
deader'n a rotten stump. You get my drift?"

Brakett pointed at his pistol belt. "Jus' might have
one other little bitty piece of 'nformation fer ya, if'n I
can have my gun back."

149

A thin-lipped frown was his only reward for the unexpected offer.

"Thank you'll fin' it right enlightnin', Marshal."

Longarm slipped Brakett's Smith & Wesson pistol from the holster he'd draped over his shoulder and ejected all the bullets. The tossed rig landed in Brakett's lap.

"Get on with it. What else have you got to say?"

Brakett leaned forward as though about to tell an important secret. In a hushed voice, he said, "Didn't jes' go to Springtown fer uh new twitsh, Marshal. Said he'd heard Doc Caine and his brother Ezra might be there sommers, too. Said if'n they wuz, he 'uz a-gonna hire 'em an' come on into Fort Worth with 'em."

"The Caine brothers. Interestin'. Why would he want to talk with that pair of killers?"

"Ain't sure. We're pert low on fun these days. Ain't had no work in quite a spell. An' . . ."

"And what, goddammit? Get on with it if you've got anything else to say."

Brakett swallowed hard, then rubbed a finger across his damaged gums. His speech improved a bit when he said, "Well, he's mighty pissed 'bout how you went and pistol-whipped 'im in the White Elephant. You are the one what done that, ain't you?"

Longarm leaned against the wall, pulled out two cheroots, and handed one to Brakett. He struck a lucifer, lit Brakett's, then his own. As he shook the flame to death, he said, "You think Quincy's makin' plans to rid the planet of my shadow? Is that what you're tryin' to tell me?"

Brakett pulled his smoking cheroot from between bloody lips. "Ain't no thinker, Marshal. Jes' tellin' you what he said. You do with the information what you will. But you'd best be a-thinkin' on this particular fact, for sure. The Caine brothers and Quincy go back a good many years. Been friends as long as I can 'member. If'n he finds 'em boys, and if'n they come back to Fort Worth with 'im, you can bet 'at 'ere bone-handled Colt of yer'n that they's gonna be a-lookin' fer you. And when they finds you, bet they's gonna be a killin'."

"Appreciate the warnin', Silas," Longarm said, and then heeled it for the hallway. Over his shoulder he added, "But that don't change your situation with me. Get outta town and be damned quick about it."

Brakett rose on unsteady legs. He picked an errant sprig of tobacco from his swollen lower lip, then flicked it onto the bed. Under his breath, as he stumbled through the Preston girls' door, he mumbled, "Yeah, I'm a-goin', you mean-assed son of a bitch." He fingered at his empty gums again. "Hope Quincy kills you and that other bastard deader'n a pair of rotten stumps."

Chapter 15

In a garbage-littered, aromatic alleyway, across a dusty and rutted Throckmorton Street from Fort Worth's Drover's Inn, Longarm leaned against the board-and-batten wall of a busy Chinese restaurant named Fong's Golden Palace. The ramshackle building was neither golden nor a palace, but that didn't appear to matter much. Hungry customers came and went at a constant and bustling pace. While watching for any indication of possible threat, Longarm absentmindedly flipped open the loading gate on his Frontier model Colt. He half-cocked the pistol and rolled the cylinder, click by click, eyeing each round one at a time.

Overhead, a molten sun boiled away in a crystalline, cloudless sky. Waves of shimmering heat appeared to ooze up from every flat surface available to the eye. Long-arm holstered the pistol, pulled his hat off, then wiped his sweaty forehead with an already saturated bandanna. Seemed as though the sun had determined to auger its way through his snuff-colored Stetson and into his skull.

The sweltering deputy marshal shifted a chewed cheroot from one corner of his dry mouth to the other.

Almost to himself, he muttered, "Feels like we're sittin' in a fryin' pan. Can't believe it's this hot so early in the year."

A bit farther down the alley, Willard Allred lay in the bed of his wagon. Long, bony legs dangled over the edge of the lowered tailgate. Badly booted feet dragged the ground. He'd pulled a ragged slouch hat down to cover his face. He raised the bottom half of the hat, then said, "Aw hell, it ain't hot, Marshal Long. Not yet. Cain't be more'n ninety. Jus' *seems* like a hunnert an' ten."

"Damnation, Willard, been here since daylight and ain't seen nothin'. Enough to make a man think there ain't much of anybody even a-stayin' at the Drover's. Ain't near the traffic around this part of town, is there? Don't even compare with the constant, seething mob trampin' up and down the streets on the north end of town near the White Elephant."

"Not much to attract folks down this way, Marshal. Town kinda plays out. Ain't nothin' a few blocks west of here but the real wild, wild West. Men like Ballentine like it that way. Why most of 'em find rooms in places like the Drover's."

"I'm sure you're right."

"You know, we could be here all day. Hell, you know as well as I do, Silas Brakett's a known liar, cheat, thief, and scoundrel. Son of a bitch just might've sent us out on a wild-goose chase. Wouldn't surprise me a bit to discover he's sprawled out at a table in the Matador Saloon down in Waco, a-laughin' his stupid, worthless ass off."

Longarm snatched the mangled cheroot from his mouth, then spit. "You've givin' the man far more credit for smarts than he's got comin', Willard. Bet if you

154

could put Brakett's brain in a grasshopper, the poor beast would hop backward."

"So, you still believe 'im?"

"He didn't have any good reason to lie. Didn't have any cause to even tell me about this business. Way I got it figured, he thought partin' with the information might get him a reprieve from my hot-mouthed admonishment to get the hell outta town."

"Reckon him and Cobb actually left, Marshal?"

"They damn well better have. I'm not given to makin' idle threats."

Allred sat up, then stuffed the tattered hat back on his sweaty head. "Never figured you wuz, Marshal. But two-tailed skunks like Cobb and Brakett sometimes hold to a strange sense of loyalty. Met more'n my share of 'em kinda boys whilst in that Yankee prison durin' the war. Learned pert quick it warn't a good idea to trust anythin' such bastards said and very little of what they did. Men like Brakett'll say anythang to get out of a pinch, then stab you in the back first chance what comes around."

Longarm ambled back to the wagon, climbed up on the tailgate, and flopped down beside Allred. For the next several hours they sat, smoked, napped, talked, and even ate some of the exotic and strange food Willard got at Fong's.

Half a dozen different kinds of exotic delicacies came wrapped in bits of brown paper. Longarm bit into one of the mysterious treats, chewed it up, swallowed, then said, "What the hell'd you call this thing?"

"Uh, that'uns a fried egg roll. Tasty, ain't it?"

"Ain't half bad. Wonder how well they'd travel in a saddlebag."

Willard shook his head. "Not too good. 'Bout ten minutes, at best. Get to stinkin' pert quick-like. Gotta eat 'em soon's you get 'em. I've noticed as how they have a tendency to go kinda mushy once they cool off."

Longarm sucked a flavorsome finger, then said, "You eat here often?"

"Yeah, it's cheap for what you get. I like it. 'Sides, Mr. Fong's a damned nice feller. Always glad to see me. Treats me a lot nicer'n some restaurant owners here in town. 'Sides that, he makes the best Chinky food in this part of Texas."

Willard wadded the empty paper wrappings from their meal into a tight lump, then pitched it over his shoulder. He glanced into the street. A party of horsemen slowly ambled toward the Drover's. "Look there, Marshal. Ain't that Quincy yonder? Sure looks like 'im to me."

Longarm hopped off the wagon bed and, with Willard right behind, heeled it to the alley's entrance, stopped at the corner, then intently gazed across the street. He watched as Ballentine reined up in front of the hotel and climbed off a long-legged bay mare. A pair of young, confused-looking, cherry-cheeked females riding double on a line-backed dun moved in beside Ballentine. The man made quite a display of gallantly helping each girl from her mount. Last to arrive at the hitch rail were two heavily armed men Longarm recognized as the Caine brothers.

He tilted his head toward Allred and, in a barely audible voice, said, "Appears as how Quincy's recruited *two* girls to take Mattie's place. Cute little things, aren't they?"

"Mighty young, too. God Almighty, jus' cain't imag-

156

ine what in the wide world the man must whisper in a unspoiled gal's ear to get 'em to go a-whorin' in a hell-hole like the Acre."

"Sad circumstance, any way you slice it. Maybe we can correct the situation before their dilemma gets outta hand. By the way, them's the Caine boys a-bringin' up the rear."

"Which one's which?" Willard whispered in Long-arm's ear.

"Doc's the tallest of the pair. Wearin' the flat-brimmed Boss of the Plains hat and sportin' the silver-plated Colt stuck in his belt backward—Hickok style. Features him-self quite the gunhand, from what I've heard. Little brother Ezra's the runty one. Looks almost like a minia-ture version of Doc, don't he? But we mustn't underesti-mate the rat-faced little weasel. Way I've heard it, he might well be more dangerous than Doc. Some say Ezra has near a dozen notches carved into the grips of his pistols."

"We gonna brace 'em now, Marshal? Take Quincy in tow, drag him into an alley, and thump his ass good for what he went and done to Miss Wayland?"

"No, not yet." Longarm ran a hand over his stubble-covered chin, then scratched a spot on the side of his jaw. He watched as Ballentine's tiny band disappeared inside the Drover's Inn. "Too dangerous for the women, Willard. Wouldn't want to confront the skunk and maybe start up a gunpowder dance that might end with a wall of lead in the air that gets one of 'em hurt, or worse."

"Well, how we gonna handle the situation?"

"There's chairs on either side of the hotel's front door. See 'em?"

"Yeah, I see 'em."

"Think we'll just stroll on over, take a seat on the boardwalk, and wait for Quincy and his friends to come back outside. Be willin' to wager we won't be a-seein' the girls on the street with any of 'em boys again. We'll keep our hats pulled down and our collars turned up. They won't even notice us. And since Quincy don't know you, that'll give us somethin' of an advantage. Hell, we might get lucky. Maybe Quincy'll come back outside alone."

Allred spit, levered a fresh shell into the chamber of his rifle, then eased the hammer down. "Gonna confront 'em soon's they hit the porch again?"

Longarm moved into the street with Willard at his heel. "If they do come out, wait till they get into the street. Tell you what, just take a seat and follow my lead. Don't do anything till you see me give you the sign. Got that?"

"Every word."

Nigh on an hour later, Longarm squirmed in the uncomfortable cane-bottomed chair next to the Drover's Inn's front entrance and glanced over at Allred. The old soldier's chin rested on his chest, and he appeared to have fallen asleep. *Can't blame him,* Longarm thought, *didn't expect this to take so long*. He fished another cheroot from his vest pocket and jammed it into his mouth. As he scratched a match to life, cupped his hands around the flame, and leaned over to light the smoke, Doc Caine and brother Ezra stepped onto the boardwalk, then swaggered into the street. Allred snapped to attention, but Longarm quickly waved for him to stay put.

Doc Caine clapped an arm over his brother's shoulders. From behind the pair, Longarm heard the man say,

"Stick with Quincy, Ezra, and we'll always be knee-deep in the best pussy in Texas. Man sure knows how to pick 'em, don't he?"

The shorter of the two dangerous ruffians threw his head back and let out an odd, snorting, insane laugh. "'At 'ere lil' black-haired thang came nigh on rippin' my whanger right off. Fought like a branded tiger. Gal damn near wore me out, I'll tell ya."

The clueless pair's conversation soon turned into a jumble of unintelligible phrases as they got farther from the hotel's front entrance. Longarm and Willard continued to watch until the unsuspecting men strutted down Eighth Street and turned into the Empress Saloon.

Willard glanced over at Longarm and hissed, "Quincy's alone now, Marshal. Let's go on in an' take 'im. Drag his sorry ass out into the alley and beat the runny shit out of 'im. Make 'im wish he'd never laid a finger on that little gal up in the doc's office. Get this whole dance all the hell over with."

In a flash Longarm was on his feet. Willard followed as they made their way into the drab, shabby lobby and up to the primitive desk. A single hallway at the far end of the desk led to the tiny hostel's rooms. A skinny, greasy-haired, hawk-nosed clerk recoiled when Longarm reached across the desk and twirled the registration ledger around so he could read it.

Allred tapped the desk's rough-cut top with the barrel of his Winchester. "Which room is Quincy Ballentine in, Vern?"

The clerk's head snapped back as though he'd been slapped. With feigned righteousness he said, "What the hell business is that of yours, Tater? Don't remember sendin' for you and your fuckin' wagon."

Longarm's finger stopped on a line in the ledger. He glanced up at the clerk. His normally friendly blue-gray eyes zeroed in like the twin muzzles of Colt .45s. "Rooms number four and five, according to your book. That right—Vern?"

"Who the hell are you?" the clerk snorted back.

"He's a deputy U.S. marshal, Vern. Answer the man," Allred growled.

Poor Vern looked confused. He fidgeted with the book as though halfheartedly trying to pull it out of Longarm's grasp. "Well, okay, okay. Yeah. Mr. Ballentine rented two rooms. Brought some girls in here 'bout an hour ago. Country girls, from the look of their dress. Had some other fellers with him, but they left."

Longarm leaned over the desk top until his hat brim almost touched the clerk's nose. "Which room is Ballentine in right now, Vern?"

"Far as I'm aware, number four. Has one of them girls in there with him. Think the other'n is alone in room five. She just got finished servicin' them two friends of Mr. Ballentine's 'fore they left."

"How would you know that, Vern?" Allred asked.

The clerk swelled up like an insulted toad. "Walls are so thin in this place, ain't much of anythin' goes on here I don't know about. Hell, Marshal, that gal was squealin' like a stuck pig the whole time. Wonder folks passin' on the street didn't hear it."

Longarm slipped his pistol from its cross-draw holster. "Which side of the hall is number four on, Vern?"

"Right. Second door down on the right. Number five is catty-cornered across the hall on the left."

Longarm crept away from the desk and into the narrow, stuffy passageway. Willard followed so close he could feel the man's ragged breath on his neck. From behind them, Longarm heard the clerk call out, "For the love of Christ, try not to break anything. Owner'll blame me for it if'n you do. Make me pay."

At the second door on the right, Longarm waved Willard to a halt. He snatched his hat off and placed an ear against the battered plank portal. He shook his head, then stuffed the hat back on. He motioned Willard around him, then whispered, "We'll hit the door at the same time. Should be quite a surprise when we bust in."

Willard's eyes got big. "Try the knob," he hissed. "Worked before."

Longarm twisted the knob, but the door wouldn't give. He motioned Willard to the far wall, silently counted to three with his fingers, then both men shouldered the door at the same time. The frame groaned, then split with a thunderous cracking noise. Rendered wood burst into a shower of splinters that shot from around the bolt of the cheap lock. The door flew open and bounced off the interior wall like a pistol shot.

Rifle at the ready, Willard made his way into the room a step ahead of Longarm and stumbled to a stunned stop at the foot of the bed. Ballentine was nowhere to be seen. Spread-eagled across a filthy, blood-stained mattress a wide-eyed, gagged, stark-naked girl bucked and twisted against rawhide thongs that bound her hands and feet to the iron posts of the bed.

"Jesus," Willard said. He propped his rifle against the bed, then went to work on the girl's bindings with a knife he fished from his boot. He freed her feet first, then her arms, which fell to her sides as though she'd lost any controlled use of them.

Longarm grabbed a discarded blanket from the filthy

floor and threw it over the bruised, nude body. He picked at the knotted gag, then lifted it away from her battered face. He ran a comforting hand across the girl's forehead and smoothed sweaty hair away from her eyes.

"Can you speak, miss?" he asked.

She nodded, then worked at it, but for several seconds couldn't get the words to come out.

"Take your time. We're here to help." Willard offered, then patted the beaten girl on the shoulder.

In a rough, barely perceptible whisper she finally gasped, "Where's my sister?"

Longarm glanced at Willard, then said, "Stay here. I'll check the other room. Anyone comes through this door but me, don't hesitate, shoot 'em."

In a rush of noise that sounded like a West Texas cyclone raging, Longarm charged across the hallway, hit the door to room number five, and turned it into a pile of kindling. He stumbled across the room and ricocheted off the iron bedstead before regaining his balance. The scene before the astonished lawman took his breath away.

"Christ Almighty," he breathed. An unconscious, black-haired girl, who couldn't have been any more than fourteen years old, lay across the bed. For several seconds he thought she might be dead. A scarlet puddle of drying gore that testified to her recently taken virginity spread from the spot between splayed, limp legs. Knife cuts and ugly pricked spots decorated her inner thighs and belly. Bloody handprints decorated the child's pale arms and legs, and were smeared across her badly bruised body.

Longarm turned his pistol toward the noise coming from the hallway. Willard Allred stood in the rendered door and gasped. "Good God. Thought I'd seen the worst of it. Shit, she ain't nothin' more'n a child, Marshal Long. Ain't even tied like the other girl. Bet them Caine boys done this'un."

"Thought I told you to . . . ah hell, it doesn't matter. Go get your wagon. We gotta get both these girls to Doc Wheeler's office quick as we can."

"Whatta ya think happened to Quincy?"

Longarm shook his head. "Best I can come up with is he probably went out the back way. Now go get the wagon, this can't wait."

Willard nodded. "Be right back," he snapped, then stormed down the hallway like a cyclone.

In a frenzy of bustling noise and action, Longarm and Allred moved the two damaged females out of the rooms, through the Drover's Inn's lobby, and into Willard's wagon.

During the entire noisy fracas, the hotel's desk clerk dithered around them, got in the way, and squealed, "Swear to Jesus, I didn't know nothin' about none of this. Never heard nothin' outta the ordinary. 'Cept maybe a bit of what I'd call girly squeals of pleasure. You know what I mean?"

Longarm laid the girl from room four in the bed of the wagon, then turned on the clerk and said, "Get the hell away from me, you spineless piece of shit. You might not've known *exactly* what was happenin', but ain't no way you didn't have a pretty fair idea. Makes me sick just lookin' at you."

He hopped onto the seat beside Allred. "Whip 'em up, Willard. Not sure how bad the one I found is hurt. 'Sides, we don't get away from here fast I'm gonna kick hell outta that stupid fuckin' clerk."

Chapter 16

Doctor John Wheeler stepped from the larger of his private examining rooms, then eased the door closed behind him. He ran a trembling hand through thinning hair. As though lifting an anvil, he pulled the stethoscope from around his birdlike neck, and shook his head. He glanced around the crowded office. His fleeting looks skittered from the tired faces of Marshal Sam Farmer and a pair of Fort Worth's policemen, over to Willard Allred, and finally hesitated on Custis Long.

"Well, what's the verdict?" Long snapped.

Wheeler strode across the congested room, placed a hand on Longarm's shoulder, and ushered him onto the boardwalk. He pulled the door closed behind them for some privacy. As they stood on the edge of the rough walkway, Wheeler let out a tired sigh, then said, "You got an extra cheroot on you, Marshal?"

Longarm fished a square-cut stogie from his vest pocket. He fired a match and watched as the haggard-looking sawbones puffed the cigar to life.

Wheeler leaned back on his heels, sent blue-gray smoke toward the darkening sky, then said, "Actually, their condition isn't quite as bad as it first appeared, Marshal. I know they looked pretty rough when you brought 'em in. But the truth is, other than being roughly treated beyond describing, held down, and havin' the hell raped out of 'em, neither girl has suffered through nearly the kind of severe beating Miss Wayland did. Recovery for these young ladies is simply a matter of a few days' rest and recuperation. Youngest of 'em appears to have suffered the most damage. Have to admit, the flower of her innocence was rather forcefully taken from her."

"Find out what their names are, Doc?"

"Poleman, I believe. Oldest girl's name is Anita. Younger one's called Martha. Near as I was able to ascertain, they're from a family livin' over around Springtown."

"That fits with information Willard and I forced out of an associate of Ballentine's named Brakett. Wish now I'd have squeezed him a mite harder. Did either girl say why they made the mistake of comin' to Hell's Half Acre with Ballentine in the first place?"

"Miss Anita said the man made claims to the rather lofty positon of impresario. Said he had ties and great influence at the Centennial Theater and the Theatre Comique. Told 'em their beauty and obvious talent would ensure a spot onstage. Guess it's easy to put stars in a country girl's eyes. We certainly see plenty of disillusioned young women down in the Acre."

Longarm spat in disgust, then snapped, "Damned shame, if you ask me."

Doc Wheeler rubbed his forehead with the back of his hand. "Have you by any chance got the impression

this whole incident might've been staged for your bene-
fit, Marshal?"

"What? What the hell does that mean, Doc?"

"Just thinking out loud."

Longarm shook his head, then cast a darting glance
into the busy thoroughfare. "No. I don't believe that for
a second. 'Course, I suppose someone at the White Elephant could've told him who I am—my lawman's background and such. No, still don't believe it. There's just
not any way Quincy's that smart."

"Sons of bitches are oftentimes smarter'n we like to
think."

"Look, Doc, I can understand why, and how, he
caught Mattie out in the street and beat hell out of her.
But his treatment of these girls was simply the kind of
behavior you can expect from an abusive pimp in the
process of conditioning new women for his own nefarious and exploitative ends. Me'n Willard just happened
to break in on the whole mess before it had a chance to
go any further. Lord knows what the Poleman girls
would've looked like a week from now if we hadn't
stepped in on 'em when we did."

Wheeler took a deep drag off his cigar. He blew the
smoke skyward again. "Don't doubt your assessment a
bit, Marshal. Please believe that my question was nothing more than the random musings of an inquisitive
mind. Whole business just seems a mite coincidental,
don't you think? I mean, you'd had contact with Miss
Wayland before her brutal beating, and then you go and
find the Poleman girls after they'd been terribly mis-
treated by the same man."

Longarm glared at the Fort Worth physician. "Well,

167

you can believe me when I tell you, Doc, he won't get a chance to do anything like this again."

Both men turned to face City Marshal Sam Farmer when he stepped onto the boardwalk with them. "We have anywhere from two to five soiled doves a year who die right here in the Acre, Marshal Long," Farmer said. "Some by their own hand, others at the hands of passing, drunken cowboys. And every once in a while, as was almost the case in this instance, an irate pimp kills one of 'em."

"Dangerous work, that's for sure," Wheeler said.

Farmer nodded. "Sellin' her body to strangers is a hard life for any woman. If the alcohol, drugs, or disease don't get 'em, depression, suicide, or murder probably will."

Longarm shifted his stance, then leaned against a porch pillar. "You're not tellin' me anything I don't already know, Sam. But what we've got here is the brutal attempted murder of one woman, and the wicked, unconscionable abuse of two others—one of whom appeared to be an untouched virgin, pure as the driven snow in Montana. Now, I don't know about anyone else, but I'm gonna have Willard searchin' in every crack and cranny of the Acre for Quincy Ballentine and the Caine boys. And God have mercy on their collective sorry asses when we find 'em—'cause I've hit the end of my string with the whole sorry bunch. Got no use for men who'll abuse women like this."

Farmer pushed his hat back and scratched his head. He yanked the hat down low over his eyes, then said, "We'll be lookin' as well. Can't have this kind of heartless brutality happenin' on my watch. Gonna take everything I can do just to keep it out of the damned newspapers.

Scribblin' sons of bitches get hold of a story like this, it'll be weeks 'fore they turn it loose."

Longarm's pointed stare bored in on Farmer. "You're not gonna let the tale get out?"

"Not if I can stop it. Kind of story has the power to destroy just about any elected lawman who ever pinned on a badge. No, we'll find Ballentine, and the others, and deal with them ourselves."

"Not if I find 'em first," Longarm snorted. "I'm gonna put Willard on their trail and, sure as God made little green apples, I'd bet he finds Ballentine and the Caine boys by mornin'."

The sun had been up for almost three hours the next day, and no word had yet arrived from Willard Allred. Longarm lounged in his favorite brocaded chair in the El Paso Hotel's busy lobby. Loaded and ready for instant use, his ten-gauge Greener stood discreetly propped against the wall behind a dainty, curve-legged, walnut table next to the overstuffed seat. He nursed a big mug of dark, viscous, aromatic coffee from the nearby bar and scanned a copy of that morning's *Fort Worth Daily Gazette*. True to his word, it appeared Marshal Sam Farmer had kept any mention of Mattie Wayland's brutal beating, or the equally vicious attack on the Poleman girls, from appearing in the paper.

He'd just folded the town's favorite rag and closed his eyes for a second when Willard hustled up with a toothy grin on his face. "Found 'em, Marshal Long. Found all of 'em."

Longarm sprang to his feet, stuffed his hat on, then grabbed the shotgun. "Where? Where are they?"

"Well, they're right across the street, over by the

White Elephant. Been askin' questions of anyone who'll stand still long enough. Tryin' to find you, actually."

"That a fact?"

"Yep. Tell ya, it's been a helluva night, Marshal. Tracked 'em all the way from the Empress Saloon, where we last seen the Caine boys, down to the Emerald. They went from the Emerald to the Headlight Bar on Ninth. Sons of bitches drank up everthang they could lay a lip on. They got right belligerent in their travels, too. Picked a fight damn near ever' place they stopped. Nobody stupid enough to accommodate 'em, though. Rogued around all night long from one waterin' hole to the next. Kept steady movin' north."

"That's how they ended up right outside?"

"Who knows? There's rumors all over the Acre 'bout how somebody come and spirited them two girls outta the Drover's Inn. Ballentine's been a-slingin' it around durin' his travels as how he's gonna kill the hell outta whoever stole his *property.* Could be as how the clerk at the Drover's told Ballentine and the Caines who spirited them little gals away, and it just took 'em all night to finally build up enough liquor-fueled nerve to finally get up here."

"Stole his property?"

"Yep. Get the impression as how old Quincy harbors pretty strong feelin's on the issue. He feels like he owns them gals."

Longarm cracked the shotgun open, pulled out each load and examined it, then snapped the weapon shut and propped it on his hip. "Say they're outside in the street?"

"Well, they wuz over on the corner, hangin' 'round the entrance to the White Elephant. Think maybe durin' his searchin' last night, Ballentine finally also made some kind of connection between the feller what pistol-whipped his sorry ass in Luke Short's restaurant, and the marshal who took them girls of his'n what disappeared."

"Surprised he didn't recognize you, given that the clerk at the Drover's knows you a lot better'n he knows me."

"Figured the same thing, so I stayed outta sight much as I could. Didn't give 'em the opportunity to spot me."

Longarm glanced across the lobby at the El Paso Hotel's front entrance. "You up for the possibility of a blisterin' gunfight, Willard?"

A wide grin flashed across Allred's bedraggled, friendly face. "Born ready, Marshal Long. Especially when there's the possibility I can put right some of the horrors carried out on them poor young women by bastards like Ballentine and the Caine brothers."

"You see any of Marshal Farmer's Fort Worth policemen on the street 'fore you came in here?"

"Not a single one. Typical of their behavior, though. Gutless sons of bitches tend not to be around when a body really needs 'em. 'Specially if'n there's the possibility of hot lead a-fillin' up the air."

Longarm slapped the old Confederate soldier on the shoulder. "We don't need 'em, Willard. Just wanted to make sure they're not around to meddle, or get in the way."

"Well, then, let's go round this bunch of woman-abusin' bastards up, or send 'em to the devil's doorstep, if'n we're forced to, by God."

"Once we get out on the street, we'll get as close to the trio as we can, and I'll try to arrest 'em. Turn 'em over to Farmer and let local law take its due course, if'n they're willin' to throw down their weapons. But if that don't work, they'll likely fight. Shootin' starts, I want you to go for Quincy. Aim for the biggest part of 'im with that rifle of yours. I'll use the shotgun on the Caine boys. Figure they'll stick fairly close to each other and make a good target. All of that clear enough?"

Allred grinned, then levered a live round into the chamber of his rifle. "Go on ahead, Marshal. Cut 'er loose and let 'er buck."

Chapter 17

Longarm strode onto the rough plank walkway in front of the El Paso Hotel. Like an obedient pet, Willard Allred followed. A hot, dust-laden wind blew past them and swept east along Third Street toward Calhoun. Allred stepped up to a spot alongside Longarm, then snapped a brusque nod to indicate the location of their prey.

Directly across Third, near a hitch rail on the south side of the White Elephant, Quincy Ballentine and the Caine brothers railed at those passing by. As if by some magical transference of thought, Ballentine and his cohorts turned in unison, exchanged a few quick words, then moved into the middle of the street. They faced Longarm and Allred and assumed a belligerent, unyielding stance.

A cold, prickling sensation, accompanied by a pimply patch of chicken flesh, crawled up Longarm's spine into his hairline at the base of his skull. "Shit," he muttered under his breath. "Sharpen up, Willard. Looks to me like these sons of bitches intend on a-goin' down shootin'."

Alert onlookers up and down the busy thoroughfare spotted the heavily armed threat and headed for the nearest available spot perceived as offering safety. Doors, alleyways, shops, and stores soon filled with anxious, finger-pointing spectators who appeared convinced a killing was about to take place.

Ballentine, a nasty abrasion still decorating his bruised jaw, spit, then kicked dust onto the gob of phlegm. "For some reason, I figured you jus' might be the son of a bitch I was a-lookin' to find." He ran a thumb along the scab-covered scrape left by Custis Long's pistol barrel. "Ain't forgot what you done to me right in front of God, Mattie, and everybody in the White Elephant, you arrogant bastard. Hear tell you're some kinda federal fuckin' lawdog."

"Deputy U.S. marshal, as a matter of pure fact. You boys are all under arrest."

Doc Caine threw his head back and let out an odd, strangled, cackling laugh. "You can fold yore arrest five ways and stick it right straight up yore dumb fuckin' ass. Ya know, I ain't never kilt no *federal* lawman afore. 'Course they's a first time for everthang." Rock-steady hands hovered over the butts of the pistols that poked from the red sash around his waist.

Brother Ezra, thumbs hooked over his cartridge belt, moved several steps away from his brother's side. "Don't think you and that broke-down old reb've got the stones to arrest boys as bad as us, Mr. Deputy U.S. Fuckin' Marshal. You ain't dealin' with a couple a ignorant, South Texas brush poppers just up from the Nueces River country chasin' a herd a them stinkin'-assed longhorns."

With Willard in tow, Longarm moved off the boardwalk, then took several more steps toward the trio of swaying-in-the-wind drunks. The action brought him and his specially appointed deputy within fifteen or twenty feet of Ballentine and the obviously inebriated Caine brothers.

Longarm leveled the shotgun and cocked it. The loud, metallic snap from the weapon's hammers being set caused a bleary-eyed Doc Caine to rock back on his heels.

Quincy Ballentine held up a conciliatory hand, as though to slow the action a bit. "Now just a second there, lawdog. You've got property what belongs to me. Bought and paid for, if you get my drift. All I really want is to get my rightful belongin's. Gimme back them girls you took from the Drover's Inn and we'll just let this whole misunderstandin' pass. Nobody'll get hurt."

Allred snarled, "You cain't buy and sell people no more, you stupid son of a bitch. Lotta good men died in Mr. Lincoln's war to prove that. Just cause these'uns happen to be women don't make it right for you to do it."

Ballentine's face reddened. He shook his finger at the lawmen. "Them Poleman gals is mine. Paid for in gold coin. Bought 'em from their dear, sweet, lovin' pappy. Even hear tell you've got Mattie as well. Some surprised she ain't dead, but I want her back, too."

Sharp-eared spectators to Third Street's unfolding events had trouble hearing Longarm when he growled, "I've heard enough of this bilge. Throw up your hands, you woman-beatin' sons of bitches. I'll not allow stupid, abusive scum like you to spend another moment a-breathin' the sweet air of God's freedom."

True to Longarm's prediction, Ezra Caine opened the ball by going for the pistol on his hip. His first shot zipped past Longarm's ear like a Mexican hornet, his second sawed across the stolid lawman's upper arm and left a smoking trench in his snuff-colored suit jacket. Doc Caine managed to get both pistols working and ripped off four quick, thunderous blasts, but the evening's whiskey consumption appeared to have spoiled his aim. Blue whistlers bored through the air all around Longarm and Allred, but did no damage.

From the corner of his eye, Longarm spotted Willard Allred as, with great deliberation, the old soldier dropped to one knee, took aim, and calmly drilled Quincy Ballentine dead center. The shot crushed the belligerent pimp's breastbone, augered its way through his body, then burst out his back in a melon-sized spray of blood, bone, and gore.

In the midst of the hot but harmless barrage coming his way from the Caine boys, Longarm dropped the hammer on both barrels of the Greener he held at waist level. A deafening roar from the weapon produced a massive, devastating curtain of lead that splattered the brothers with hundreds of heavy-gauge buckshot pellets. Both men disappeared from sight behind a gray-black cloud of spent gunpowder that rolled across the span of dusty street between the two parties and virtually obscured anyone's ability to see his adversaries.

Longarm pitched the shotgun aside, slipped the Frontier model Colt from its cross-draw holster, and advanced on the three fallen gunnies. He marched through the drifting, acrid haze he'd put in the air and stopped a few feet from the twitching body of Doc Caine. Smoking buckshot holes that oozed blood adorned the man's clothing from his knees to his chin. He groaned and sat up, a pistol in each hand.

"Drop 'em, Doc," Longarm warned.

Caine's eyes swam in his head. A number of black-ringed holes peppered his face and neck. "Gonna send you to hell, you badge-wearin' son of a bitch. Ain't nobody done ever shot me and lived to tell of it."

With what appeared every bit of strength he had left, Caine partially raised one arm and fired a shot that knocked a heel off Longarm's boot and sent the surprised marshal to his knee. On his way to ground, the astonished lawman snapped off a single round that hit Caine over the right eye, knocked the Boss of the Plains hat off his head, and snatched him backward into the dirt like he'd been roped for branding.

Longarm hopped back to his feet like a man trying to disguise the fact that he'd fallen in public, then quickly drew a death-dealing bead on brother Ezra. The younger of the brothers appeared to have got the worst of the initial blast from the Greener. He shuffled up to Ezra and toed the man in the side. The wounded gunman groaned, but only once. Willard Allred stepped up beside Longarm and, without even taking aim, fired a single shot into the downed man's chest.

Longarm holstered his pistol as Willard levered a fresh load into the Winchester's smoking breech. "Know you probably don't approve of what I just done, Marshal, but the way I've got it figured, ain't no point lettin' any of 'em take up space in a jail. Besides, gutless juries 'round here'bouts have a bad habit of lettin' his type loose on the public with little or no punishment for their nefarious deeds," Allred said.

Longarm stared down at Ezra Caine's lifeless body. Dung flies had already begun to buzz around the man's corpse. "Good thing he, at the very least, had a weapon in hand. Mighta looked kinda bad otherwise."

Allred ambled over to the corpse of Quincy Ballentine. He toed the body onto its back, bent over, and rifled through the dead man's pockets. After several seconds, he stood, held out a bulging leather pouch, and said, "Look. Must be a couple a thousand dollars in here, Marshal Long."

Longarm gazed at his own feet, then turned away as though trying not to hear what Allred was saying. He pinched the bridge of his nose, then made a waving motion behind his back. "Put it in your pocket, Willard. Quincy don't have any use for the money, and if we leave the pouch on 'im, one of Fort Worth's policemen'll probably end up with it."

Willard shoved the bag of paper money and coins into his coat pocket, then followed Longarm to the wooden walkway next to the White Elephant. They sat down next to one another and watched as scores of cowboys, tradesmen, store owners, bartenders, cattle buyers, gamblers, drunks, women of questionable background, and others gathered around, pointed, whispered, and gawked at the blood-soaked, bullet-riddled corpses that bedecked the dusty street.

Allred propped the rifle against his knee. A faint twinge of regret colored his voice when he said, "Been a right gory couple a days, Marshal. Ain't kilt this many men since the war."

Longarm glanced over at the grizzled old reb, then patted him on the shoulder. "You can take some degree of comfort in the knowledge we did what had to be done at the time, Tater. No shame in any of our actions. No shame at all."

"Suppose so," Allred mused. "Still and all, though, it's been a bloody couple a days."

In pretty short order a tall, cadaverous-looking gent lugged a heavy box camera up and efficiently went about taking as many pictures as possible. He'd set off his flash bar at least twice when Marshal Sam Farmer and one of his men appeared on the scene.

Longarm and Allred stood when Farmer strode up. Fort Worth's marshal pulled a chewed toothpick from between his teeth, then said, "Well, see you went an' beat us to 'em, Marshal Long."

"Not really," Longarm said. "They came lookin' for a fight. Appears someone told 'em 'bout me a-rescuin' the Poleman girls. Quincy didn't take the news well. Tried to get 'em to throw up their hands and let me take 'em in. Had every intention to turn 'em all over to you, Sam. You can see how the whole dance all turned out."

Farmer shook his head. Over his shoulder, as he stepped into the street for a better viewing of the shot-riddled bodies, he said, "Yeah, I can see how it turned out alright."

Willard touched Longarm's elbow, then tapped the leather bag in his pocket. "How 'bout we step inside the Elephant, and you let me buy a round of drinks."

Longarm passed a rather pleasant week in Fort Worth after the fiery dustup with Quincy Ballentine and the Caine brothers. Surprised everyone when the weather turned a bit cooler and a welcome rain settled the ever-present, drifting dust. Mornings he lounged in the El Paso Hotel's sumptuous lobby, sipped coffee, and studied the local newspapers. Around about noon every day, he and Willard Allred strolled over to the White Elephant and had lunch. Nights, Allred watched as Longarm played poker with Luke Short and a pair of former Kansas lawdogs named Bat Masterson and Wyatt Earp, who traveled in the company of a pale, sickly dentist named Holliday.

He visited with Mattie Wayland as often as possible. Her recovery proved depressingly slow and painful. Young fellow claiming kinship to the Poleman girls showed up early that second week. Said he'd fallen out with his pap over the whole sordid affair as concerned his sisters, and wanted to take the girls to a place where none of them were known. He quietly spirited the girls away late one night without giving anyone a chance to say good-bye.

Marshal Sam Farmer escorted Longarm to Fort Worth's Union Depot the morning he left town. The Denver, Texas, and Fort Worth Railroad's Baldwin engine chuffed and snorted ominous clouds of billowing steam onto the loading platform as they walked up.

Farmer shook Longarm's hand, then said, "Well, glad you got to spend at least some of your time off relaxing, Marshal. Woulda been a shame for the entire trip to have been as tangled as that first week."

Longarm flashed his pearly whites. "Enjoyed every minute of it, Sam. Hope to get back this way soon. Maybe have two whole weeks as pleasant as the one that just passed."

Longarm glanced over Farmer's shoulder and noticed Willard Allred pull up to the depot's passenger platform driving a shiny new cabriolet. Inside sat Mattie Wayland. "Excuse me, Sam. There's a lady here to see me off."

Scrubbed, shaved, and dressed in a new outfit from head to foot, a grinning Willard Allred hopped off the driver's deck, doffed his hat, and gallantly swung the cab's polished door open. "Damned nice rig, Tater."

"Seems as how I recently came into some unexpected money. Thought I'd provide my better customers with a real special ride." Allred's smile broadened. "Had the doc give them poor gals from Springtown enough to start on a different trail, as well. Felt mighty good, too."

Longarm patted the old soldier on the arm, then removed his hat and leaned beneath the sheltering hood. "Doc Wheeler know you're out runnin' the streets, Mattie?"

Still showing the effects of her terrible beating, Mattie Wayland forced a split-lipped grin, then said, "No, and you won't tell him, will you?"

" 'Course not. But I'm sure he'd be worried if he knew what you were doing."

"I know. Had to say good-bye, though. Couldn't let you leave town without making sure you knew how much I appreciate all you done for me."

"Totally unnecessary. Any man worth his salt would've done the same."

She grimaced, but leaned forward, caressed his face, then planted a tender, chaste kiss on Longarm's cheek. "No. No they wouldn't have," she whispered. "There aren't many men like you around these days, Custis."

He stood, stuffed the hat back on his head, then took her hand and kissed it. "Hope we meet again, darlin'. Sooner the better."

"Oh, we most certainly will meet again, Custis darlin'. Just as soon as I can get well enough to make it to Denver, I expect a second taste of our night at the El Paso."

Longarm bowed like a true Southern cavalier, then tipped his hat. "Ah, Mattie darlin', I'm an easy man to find." He flashed a broad smile, "Hell, darlin', I'm just 'by God' easy, period."

Watch for

**LONGARM AND THE
COLORADO MANHUNT**

the 349th novel in the exciting LONGARM
series from Jove

Coming in December!

GIANT-SIZED ADVENTURE FROM AVENGING ANGEL LONGARM.

BY TABOR EVANS

2006 GIANT EDITION

LONGARM AND THE OUTLAW EMPRESS
978-0-515-14235-8

2007 GIANT EDITION

LONGARM AND THE GOLDEN EAGLE SHOOT-OUT
978-0-515-14358-4

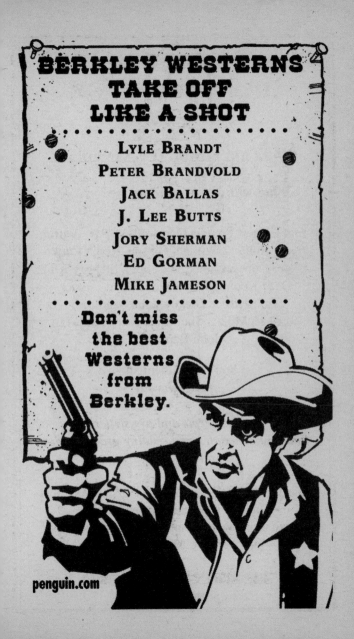